"Come to bed…" Edie murmured

Jimmy paused in the doorway. "I'm enjoying the view." His gaze was as warm as the candlelight that fluttered on his skin, and it was fixed where she was lying, propped against pillows piled high against the headboard.

She smiled. "I don't know what I'd have done without you the past week and a half."

He merely shrugged. He was shirtless, his muscular chest bare. He looked delicious, silhouetted in the semidarkness, a black line of wild curling hair bisecting his pecs and arrowing downward as if pointing to the most intimate part of him.

Just gazing at him made everything inside Edie ache and grow tight. She'd never felt this way about a man before.

Noticing the open bottle of champagne and two long-stemmed glasses dangling from his fingers, she frowned. "Correct me if I'm wrong, but I think that's meant for the Darden wedding."

"What did they order?" he asked, grinning. "A hundred cases?" He shrugged. "They won't miss one bottle."

She couldn't help but smile again. "You're positive about that?"

"Yeah. And this was a premeditated act," he admitted huskily. "I even chilled the bubbly a couple of hours ago." He moved into the room. "Somehow I figured we'd wind up in bed…."

Dear Reader,

I do hope you'll enjoy my last book in the BIG APPLE BRIDES trilogy for the Harlequin Temptation line! It's been fun writing about the three Benning sisters and the special, sexy men they each have met along the way.

After living in another state for some time, I recently returned to make my home in New York again. As always, I feel embraced by the sights and sounds! As far as I'm concerned, the city itself might as well be a Harlequin Temptation hunk, grabbing me by the waist, whirling me around until I'm breathless, then smacking me on the lips! Not that I wouldn't trade New York for this last hero, Jimmy Delaney!

I do hope you'll find him just as breathlessly exciting!

Watch for my next book in Harlequin Blaze, coming in 2006.

Happy reading!

Jule McBride

Books by Jule McBride

HARLEQUIN TEMPTATION
875—THE HOTSHOT*
883—THE SEDUCER*
891—THE PROTECTOR*
978—BEDSPELL
1005—SOMETHING BORROWED†
1013—NIGHTS IN WHITE SATIN†

HARLEQUIN BLAZE
67—THE SEX FILES
91—ALL TUCKED IN...

*Big Apple Bachelors
†Big Apple Brides

JULE McBRIDE

I THEE BED...

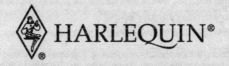

HARLEQUIN®

TORONTO • NEW YORK • LONDON
AMSTERDAM • PARIS • SYDNEY • HAMBURG
STOCKHOLM • ATHENS • TOKYO • MILAN • MADRID
PRAGUE • WARSAW • BUDAPEST • AUCKLAND

ISBN 0-373-69221-8

I THEE BED...

This edition published by arrangement with Harlequin Books S.A.

® and TM are trademarks of the publisher. Trademarks indicated with
® are registered in the United States Patent and Trademark Office, the
Canadian Trade Marks Office and in other countries.

www.eHarlequin.com

Printed in U.S.A.

1

"ALL RISE!"

"Whatever happens this time," Ches Edmond whispered, coaching his client, "keep your cool, Jimmy." As his eyes met those of the man beside him, the shared gaze held countless memories—everything from downing too many cold brewskies on fishing trips, to fighting over the same head cheerleader, to their last year of playing football together at a high school outside Cleveland. A few months after taking the team to the state finals, they'd packed their bags and moved to the Big Apple to share an East Village sublet that Jimmy had found over the Internet.

Ches added, "Judge Diana once wrote a book titled *The Wrongdoers*."

Exhaling a long-suffering sigh, Jimmy Delaney whispered, "You're kidding me, right?"

"Nope. Hit the stands a year ago last spring."

"And you didn't tell me before now?"

Ches shrugged, a two-thousand-dollar suit pulling snugly across shoulders so powerful that it looked as if he was wearing the pads from his high-school ball-playing uniform. "Did you really want to know?"

"Guess not," agreed Jimmy as he rose slowly, fighting the urge to loosen the knot of a suffocating tie, a red, white and blue monstrosity he'd bought for his parents' fortieth wedding anniversary which, had luckily fallen on July fourth, and which Jimmy now hoped would communicate his sense of patriotism to the judge.

"She's also thinking about running for public office," Ches added.

Jimmy considered. "Republican?"

"Having written *The Wrongdoers?* What do you think?"

"And for our purpose that means?"

"The harsher the sentence, the better."

"Swell," muttered Jimmy dryly. From behind him, he could feel the eyes of his other buddies, celebrity photographers who hung around The Suds Bar on Avenue A in the East Village—Benny, Alex and Tim—burning a space between his shoulders. Glancing behind himself, Jimmy rolled his eyes, showing he wasn't about to be cowed by a judge in a skirt and was pleased when he got supportive grins and a thumbs-up in response.

His spirits lifted further when he glanced at Ches again and remembered their public-speaking class in high school. The teacher, Mrs. Hepplewhite, had always said that, when nervous, you should imagine your audience naked. Easy enough in this case, Jimmy thought. Judge Diana Little might have been nearing fifty, but she took good care of herself. She had beautiful skin, and her tawny blond hair was flattering, cut to shoulder length. Even the square, black-framed glasses perched midway down her nose were kind of sexy, Jimmy decided, as he slowly, mentally removed her black robe.

Her voice, unfortunately, was hardly of the sex-kitten variety. "Mr. Delaney?"

He raised his eyebrows. "Yes, ma'am?"

"Before I sentence you, could you do me a favor?"

"Anything, ma'am. Just ask."

She sent him a quick, close-mouthed wince that was meant to be a smile. "Wipe the smirk off your face."

He should have realized Judge Diana would say something such as that. "Sorry," he muttered.

"I'm sure I'll live, Mr. Delaney," she returned curtly.

Ches whispered, "This doesn't bode well."

Judge Diana heaved a sigh, her lightly glossed lips pursing in displeasure. "And does counsel have something to say?"

"No, Judge," Ches assured.

Nodding, she stared at the top of her massive desk, her eyes roving over the contents of a three-inch-thick manila file. Very slowly, she tapped a paper with the long, slender finger of a perfectly manicured hand, causing Jimmy to bite back a sigh. Obviously, Judge Diana was going to draw out his sentencing, just to watch him squirm.

Or maybe she'd realize he'd done nothing wrong and go easy on him. He was half tempted to start speaking in his own defense; maybe if he hadn't trusted Ches's advice so much, he'd have done so already. But Ches was one of the best trial lawyers in New York City, so well-known that, if he hadn't been a friend, Jimmy wouldn't have gotten any further than a call to his assistant; despite being well employed, himself, Jimmy wouldn't have been able to afford Ches's rates, either.

Now he thanked his lucky stars for having such a talented buddy. Not only had they moved from Ohio together and finished college at NYU the same term, but Ches had gone on to law school, then made a name for himself as a defense attorney. On the first day of classes at NYU Law, he'd met a woman who was as sexy as she was brainy, and now Ches and Elsa were in their third year of married life; she'd given him two babies while joining a firm herself. The youngest child, Conner, was only three months old, but just like his older brother, Clay, he was showing signs of becoming a football star, at least as near as Jimmy and Ches could tell, even if Elsa often begged to differ.

Pushing aside the thoughts, Jimmy concentrated on Judge Diana again, wondering what was going to happen next. Ches had said it was unlikely, but Jimmy could wind up doing jail time. Jimmy sure hoped not. He glanced around. The benches in the high-ceilinged courtroom were nearly empty of people, and the place felt cavernous and smelled musty. In the silence, he could hear the ominous crackle of papers, and for the first time, he began to worry that things were about to plummet southward. Even if the sentence was harsh, Ches had said it wouldn't matter, since they'd win on appeal, but Jimmy didn't exactly relish the thought of wearing a striped uniform under any circumstances.

Regarding his legal battles, he'd long ago decided to turn his will and his life over to the care of Ches, and so, until now, he'd refused to sweat this case. It wasn't his first. Jimmy's talent was for taking pictures. From the earliest age, he'd shown a knack for color and composition, and for discovering photogenic quality in just about any subject. He could take the most seemingly homely girl in the world and make her look intriguing beyond compare. And it wasn't a trick. He'd simply been given a gift for capturing the souls of even the most elusive people. Time after time, he'd snap the shutter in the split second when a person's deepest emotions surfaced, and what might have been seen as ugly was infused with new depth. His was a talent that had brought critical acclaim when he'd first started working, and later far more than the average wage usually made by photographers.

As Judge Diana held up a copy of the *New York Post*, Jimmy braced himself for whatever sentence was to come, but she merely said, "You took this?"

He surveyed a black-and-white zoom shot of hotel heiress, Julia Darden, who'd been on the deck of a yacht sailing off the Chelsea Piers in the West Twenties. She and her fiancé, Lorenzo Santini, were wrapped in a sheet, kissing deeply, in a suggestive enough pose that any viewer would assume they were making love.

He nodded. "Yes, I did."

"And you sold it to the tabloids?"

Obviously. He tried not to balk. He was a photographer, after all. And that meant he sold his pictures. "Yes, ma'am."

"Although you knew there was an order of protection against you?"

"I was outside the court-ordered range of distance, Judge."

"A simple *yes* or *no* will do."

He sighed. "Yes. I knew there was an order."

"And not the first one Julia Darden has filed against you?"

He shook his head. "No."

"Would you want people taking pictures of you such as this?"

Jimmy should be so lucky to find himself wrapped

in a sheet, in the arms of a woman as gorgeous as Julia Darden. "I wouldn't mind in the least."

"How many orders of protection have there been?"

Honestly, he wasn't sure, so he glanced at Ches as he said, "Six or seven over the past few years. Most since she announced her wedding six months ago."

"Eleven," corrected the judge.

When she ducked her head once more and continued perusing his file, Jimmy's annoyance intensified. So maybe there had been eleven orders of protection, but Ches said he really hadn't done anything illegal, only unconventional, and with Julia Darden's wedding taking place in a couple of weeks, on April first, Jimmy could hardly afford to be in jail during the event. One picture of Julia and Lorenzo's kiss at the altar would buy him the West Village Co-op he'd been eyeing for the past year. Besides, only *Celebrity Weddings* magazine was to have access to the event, which meant getting inside would provide just the kind of challenge that Jimmy lived for.

Just thinking of the wedding, he almost smiled. Leave it to Julia Darden to name April Fools' Day for her nuptials. She definitely had a sense of humor. It was rumored that she hadn't even really wanted a ring, but only the pop-can tab with which Lorenzo had proposed, and which she now wore around her neck. She was as beautiful as she was funny, with straight brown hair, brown eyes and a wide smile, and yet, she was more than just beautiful. She had a quality Jimmy had been able to capture repeatedly on film, a projected air of having been completely well loved during all her twenty-seven years. Any hurt she might have experienced seemed to have rolled off her back, which was why she'd become one of Jimmy's—and all of America's—favorite tabloid subjects.

Her father, spry, silver-haired widower, Sparky Darden, was a character in his own right. Sixty-seven and diagnosed with cancer that had gone into remission, he was in semiretirement, enjoying an estate in Long Island where Julia's wedding was to take place. He'd spent his life building the Darden hotel empire, but he'd also spent much time doting on his daughter, giving her the life of a fairy princess, a fact that always shone through the features of her face and that, despite her aversion to cameras and publicity, had made her America's darling. Her sport star husband-to-be was no slouch, either.

But it was photographs of Julia that commanded the highest pay at the tabloids. Because she always tried to avoid publicity, Jimmy didn't understand how Emma Goldstein at *Celebrity Weddings* magazine had gotten exclusive rights to shoot the wedding. It was shocking that Julia would let anyone with a camera, much less a mainstream celebrity magazine, near the wedding, and now, despite the order of protection, Jimmy still wanted to get in the door. He was well-known among paparazzi for the inventive tactics and disguises he used to get close to subjects, but so far, Julia Darden's wedding was providing new challenges, almost daily.

It had all started last October, almost six months ago, when the wedding was first announced. Ever since, Jimmy had managed to scoop *Celebrity Weddings* by publishing shots of preparations in the tabloids, something that had brought him into contact, however anonymously, with the Benning family. As it had turned out, Julia Darden's father, because of a past association with a man named Joe Benning, had hired Joe's daughter,

Edie, as Julia's wedding planner, and Edie, prompted by *Celebrity Weddings,* had agreed to appear on a reality television show called *Rate the Dates* a couple months ago....

Jimmy had gone undercover as a videographer for *Rate the Dates,* padding his clothes, wearing a beard and calling himself Vinny Marcel. While shooting footage of Edie Benning and her date-mate, and hoping to use the ruse to get closer to Julia, he'd wound up with more of a scoop than he'd expected. As it turned out, the woman on the reality show wasn't Edie Benning after all, but rather, her twin sister, Marley, and now—assuming he wasn't going to jail—Jimmy had to come up with another game plan for getting close to Edie.

He wouldn't mind in the least. When he'd first seen the identical twin sisters together, he'd been able to tell them apart immediately. The women were identical, yes. And yet, there was something so different about their essence. Both were about five foot five. Both had worn their feathered blond hair blown straight, and both had blue eyes the color of robins' eggs on a foggy morning.

But it was Edie, not Marley, to whom he'd responded. The pull on Jimmy's body had been strangely magnetic. Unforgettable, visceral, primal. He didn't want to get to know Edie, to take her on a date, or impress her with his credentials or expertise, or even watch her eyes light up with pleasure. No...he'd awakened from dreams about her and caught himself fantasizing about loving her—quickly undressing her, stripping down her stockings, pulling down her skirt, unbuttoning the delicate blouses she favored. He could see himself pushing silk from her shoulders, exposing a white bra, the lace of which was worrying taut pink nipples that the fabric barely covered...

He suddenly blinked. Dammit, Judge Diana was staring at him, and she gave the impression she'd been doing so for some time. "Yes?" he managed.

"Did you hear a word I said, Mr. Delaney?"

With her dark eyes scrutinizing him, Jimmy decided it was probably better not to lie. "No. I'm sorry."

"Is your own sentencing boring you?"

He shook his head.

She sighed. "For your inattention alone, I should send you to Riker's Island."

Riker's Island? Ches had indicated that if Jimmy received a jail term, it would be in some cushy place for white-collar criminals. He felt Ches's hand close over his forearm, as if Ches feared Jimmy might suddenly lunge past the judge and run for freedom.

Judge Diana was eyeing him again. Using an index finger, she pushed the black-framed glasses toward the bridge of her very straight, patrician nose. "I see you studied fine art before you went into your current occupation."

What did that have to do with anything? "I was an art photographer, yes."

"And now you're pretty merciless, aren't you, Mr. Delaney? You dress in disguises, which makes it difficult to catch you in the act while you peep in windows and the like?"

"Not exactly how I'd put it." He wanted to add, "I've forgone many of the usual life pleasures, just to bring the American public the kind of pictures it most loves." Instead, he said, "I'm going to honor the order of protection, Judge." The truth was, he'd already done so, and she knew it, but the Darden's security staff and legal team were turning up the heat as the wedding day neared, hoping to keep Jimmy away from Julia.

They'd even insinuated he'd chased a Darden limousine, trying to get a shot of Julia, and that the car had swerved dangerously, but that was a blatant lie.

Yes he'd honored the order of protection, so far, but the Darden's security team was starting to pose just the kind of challenge Jimmy relished. After all, he'd done the right thing, only to be punished. Besides, he did want pictures of the wedding. *Celebrity Weddings* magazine had an exclusive, but if anybody else could get in to shoot pictures, it would be Jimmy. Suddenly, a plan began to form in his mind. Surely, there was a way to get inside the Darden estate....

Only the pounding of the gavel brought his attention back to the judge. "All and all, Mr. Delaney," she said, "I think you'll find my sentence of community service fair. You will, of course, adhere to all existent orders of protection against you. That goes without saying. In addition, beginning tomorrow at the Little Red Schoolhouse on Bleeker and Sixth Avenue, from nine o'clock until noon, and for the next six weeks, you'll meet with the shutterbugs."

Community service? What was she talking about? Pictures he'd taken of Kiefer Sutherland picking up trash along the L.A. freeway shot through his mind. Surely, he wasn't going to be wearing orange and cleaning public parks. Then the word registered. "Shutterbugs?"

Judge Diana nodded. "My juvie offenders. Believe me, I've got a bunch. This morning, an officer told me his evidence room is overflowing with camera equipment that can't be returned which was why he couldn't find some drug money for three months after he'd confiscated it. This should kill three birds with a stone."

"Three birds?" muttered Ches.

She nodded. "The officer, the kids and Mr. Delaney."

"Juvie offenders?" Jimmy managed. He'd been a lone child, and the only kids he knew lately were Ches and Elsa's sons, and they weren't even old enough to call him "Uncle Jimmy" yet. "I'm sorry, Judge, but I don't know how to teach—"

An elbow to the gut nearly took away his breath. Judge Diana, who'd seemed to catch the action, smiled. "I see your attorney, uh…" She paused, her smile broadening. "Gets the picture."

A second later, Jimmy was blinded by a series of white flashes, and in the next heartbeat, he realized his own buddies had circled to the front of the courtroom to snap his slack-jawed expression. Already, he could see the picture in the *Post* or the *Daily News.* The text would read something like, From Julia to Juvies. Didn't these guys care that selling such a photo would publicize his face, making him that much easier to spot, endangering his ability to work? "With friends like these," he muttered, "who needs enemies?"

And then thankfully, Judge Diana saved Jimmy's day by saying, "Bailiff, please confiscate all the cameras."

"THIS WEEK, YOUR ASSIGNMENT is to shoot two rolls of film, then next week, we'll start learning how to develop them in the darkroom here at the school. Are there any more questions about the basic operation of the cameras?"

The fifteen kids, ranging in age from ten to fifteen, shook their heads, and eleven-year-old Melissa Jones shuddered with pleasure. Every time she'd looked at her hero during the past three hours, she'd almost swooned. She loved tabloids, as well as watching shows like *Entertainment Tonight,* so she was completely familiar with Jimmy Delaney's work, not to mention a superfan. She'd never have expected him to be such a hunk, though. He was so supercute. Supercool, too. Even the tougher, older kids weren't giving him a hard time. She raised her hand again, just so he'd notice her. "Do we get to take the camera home today, Mr. Delaney?"

"Yes. Like I said, you're supposed to take pictures this week, okay? And you can't do that unless you take the cameras. But don't forget to be careful with the equipment. It's the property of the state."

"Yo, bro," said a kid in front of her to one of his friends. "That means we don't hawk them on Canal Street."

"That's right," agreed Jimmy. "But Chinatown would be a great place to take pictures." After turning to write a number on the blackboard, he began going from desk to desk, to double-check cameras and film. "That's my number on the board. Call me at home if you have questions."

His home number! Very carefully, Melissa copied it into her pink notebook, feeling her hands getting sweatier as he neared her desk. Setting down her pencil with shaking fingers, she slicked her palms down the sides of her jeans, shuddered, then smoothed her dark hair away from her face.

Jimmy's straight fine jet-black hair was cut very short, and even though he'd slicked it back, it stuck almost straight up, just the way Matt Damon and Ben Affleck wore theirs. He had a very square jaw, dark, liquid eyes, and a tiny dot of a mole beside his mouth.

Supersexy, Melissa thought. Yes, if she had realized that being a criminal would help her meet Jimmy Delaney, she'd have started shoplifting and maxing out her mother's credit cards on catalog shopping way back in the first grade. Suddenly, sadness twisted inside her as her mind flashed on her last arrest in Bloomingdale's. Her parents had looked so devastated. That was the word her mother had kept using—devastated.

But could Melissa help it if she was bored? And if her parents were always so mad at her?

"We've given you everything!" her mother had exclaimed between sobs, after she'd spoken with the security staff and watched her daughter on the videotape, stealing a pair of men's leather gloves. Her father, who had been a lot less kind, had said Melissa could, "forget about taking any time-outs." Both her parents had said she was a selfish girl, but Melissa didn't understand how they could have arrived at *that*. She always gave money to Jack Stevens, the homeless man who slept over the grate beneath the fire escape below her apartment. And the gloves had been for him.

Jack didn't really seem homeless, anyway. Since he was the first street person to whom Melissa had ever spoken, she'd been very surprised and had completely revised her opinion about homelessness. He'd once had a really nice apartment uptown, but after he'd lost his job, his wife had left, which was bad timing because it turned out his son needed an operation, and the insurance had lapsed, which meant the medical expenses had wiped Jack out financially. His son was better now, but he was with Jack's wife, and Jack missed them both so much that he'd started drinking, which had made things go from bad to worse. Now, Jack really thought he could turn things around if he could get into a rehab center, but treatment would cost several thousand dollars.

See? Melissa fumed. She knew all about Jack's life!

Didn't that show she was unselfish? She had what people called empathy, too. She definitely understood Jack's financial crunch. While her mother said Melissa had been given everything, it wasn't really true. Melissa wanted a horse, for instance, and she could easily relate that to Jack's feelings about his son.

She'd wanted a horse for over a year, ever since she'd seen the movie, *Black Beauty*, and when she'd asked, her father had said, "Maybe." Later, he'd gone on to say that it was more complex than just getting a horse, since they lived in New York City and would need to board it. When Melissa had suggested they move to Wyoming, her father had just laughed at her.

Well, she'd show him! Opening the back of her camera, she slowly inserted the film just as Jimmy had illustrated for the class. The key to success in business was filling a niche. She'd heard her father say it a thousand times. And now, with Jimmy Delaney gone from the paparazzi business, there was a niche to fill. Since Melissa's dad had been a linebacker for the NFL before retiring and becoming a sportscaster for a network, Melissa could get access to TV studios. The network even had an after-school program that Melissa had previously refused to attend.

Who could shoot celebrities more easily than a kid, after all? Adults never noticed kids. Melissa couldn't believe she hadn't thought of this before. If she wanted to do so, she could even get supersexy pictures in the girls' dressing rooms. If everything went as planned, she could sell the pictures, earn enough money to buy a horse, and then she wouldn't even be tempted to steal in the future.

Not that Jimmy was directly suggesting the kids should go into his line of work. But he'd chosen it, hadn't he? And that meant he'd decided it was a good job. Now, all Melissa had to do was convince Jack Stevens to help her sell the pictures she took. She'd need a grown-up to do things such as open a bank account. She could almost see the beautiful black stallion she was going to buy, and maybe...

Jimmy Delaney paused beside her desk. "What kind of pictures do you want to shoot this week, Melissa?"

When he leaned down, close to her desk, Melissa could smell a faint tinge of soap and aftershave lotion. She wanted to tell him he was so beautiful that he could be a movie star, but she only sent him a huge smile. "Close-up shots of flowers mostly," she said sweetly. "Maybe you can teach me how to make them look soft and fuzzy," she continued, trying to make her voice sound breathless. "The way they do in the art magazines." She paused. "How much money do you make when you sell things to the *Post?*"

His eyes widened. "When class began, I said I wasn't going to talk about that," he said, leaning even closer.

Her dark eyes locked with his. "Ballpark?"

For a moment, he was still, then his shoulders started shaking and he laughed. "Soft and fuzzy flowers," he repeated. "I'll be happy to give you some pointers on *that*, Melissa."

Melissa. She blew out a slow, shivery breath, barely able to believe that Jimmy Delaney—the Jimmy Delaney—had called her by her first name. Ever since the incident at Bloomingdale's, she'd been so depressed, but now life was looking up! And regarding her question about picture fees, Melissa wasn't the least bit concerned. She was a whiz on the Internet, and absolutely no information had ever eluded her.

2

"WHY DON'T WE MOVE into the front room again?" Edie Benning suggested, glancing between a dark-haired woman named Stacy LaPaglia and her husband-to-be, Reggie Hammer. The Darden wedding aside, business was slow, so Edie couldn't afford to alienate even one client. She was doing her best to be diplomatic and fulfill the couple's desires; yet, she could hardly let Stacy and Reggie remain in the conference room, perusing notes, sketches and lists pertaining to the Darden event. "Really, what we most strive to do at Big Apple Brides," Edie coaxed, "is to make each wedding absolutely unique. I want to concentrate on you and Reggie, Stacy, on any special needs you two may have as a couple, and on your own dreams and goals...."

Stacy only moved closer to the board table, grasping her fiancé's hand and dragging him with her as she lifted a sketch of Julia's gown, which Edie's mother, Viv, a seamstress, had been commissioned to help design and make. "So, this is a picture of the gown Julia Darden's wearing?"

"Uh...yes," Edie managed. "It is, but as you and Reggie probably understand, we're keeping her and Lorenzo Santini's plans as private as possible."

"But most of the preparations have been made public in *Celebrity Weddings* magazine," countered Stacy, "which is why Reggie and I are hiring you."

"I appreciate that, but..." Vaguely, Edie gestured toward the front room again, wishing these two would take the hint, so she wouldn't have to become more explicit. While what Stacy had said was true, other notes on the table pertained to less public matters, such as the security strategies for the Darden wedding, and that really was private. Thankfully, the notes involving security weren't in plain view.

"Since you do like Julia's dress," Edie ventured, "I've got a sense of your taste now, and have some others I'd like to show you. In fact, in the next room, I've got photographs I believe you'll be very interested in seeing, Stacy—"

Suddenly, Edie's heart missed a beat and her voice trailed off as she glanced through the conference-room doorway, across the reception room and through the front windows. *No one's there now.* And yet for the umpteenth time this morning, Edie sensed something amiss. Just now, she could have sworn someone had been at the windows, staring inside. She tried to take a deep breath, to calm herself, but it was no use. Her senses had gone on alert. All the colors in the room seemed brighter; the objects were outlined in sharper detail, except for Stacy and her fiancé, who might as well have vanished. Should she call the police?

Since October, shortly after Julia Darden's wedding had been announced, someone had started threatening the heiress's life. During a meeting about wedding safety, the head of the Darden's security staff, Pete Shriver, had shown Edie some of the poison-pen letters sent to Julia, and he'd even stationed a man on Edie's block for a few weeks to watch the shop, until Edie had convinced him it wasn't really necessary. Being watched around the clock had only made Edie more nervous; besides, Julia was the target, and as the wedding had neared, she'd quit coming into Big Apple Brides. Lately, Edie had been going to Long Island whenever she had business to discuss, and now, with only two weeks until the day, most preparations were taking place on the site of the event, anyway, which was the Dardens' estate.

Edie would be so glad when all this was finally over. Puffing her cheeks to blow, she exhaled, now wishing it hadn't started to snow again. The weather had been so unpredictable that she still didn't know whether to expect another blizzard or blooming spring flowers, come April first. One day last week, the temperature had hiked to seventy degrees only to plummet to thirty once more.

Well, everything's going to be fine, Edie assured herself, shaking her head to clear it of confusion. And yet, she was scared. A few weeks ago, an unidentified intruder at the Darden estate had fired gunshots while Julia and Edie's sister, Marley, had been jogging in the woods. According to Pete Shriver, the incident was probably some sort of scare tactic. As he'd put it, "If someone wants you dead, they can usually do it, Edie. But this guy's only sending letters and shooting bullets that never seem to find a human target." Pete had said that the bullets found lodged in the trees indicated the perpetrator had aimed high, which meant he hadn't really been shooting to kill.

Not that such information gave Edie comfort. She was a wedding planner, for heaven's sake. A diehard romantic. That her hearts-and-flowers business would wind up involving bodyguards had never once occurred to her.

Welcome to my life, she thought now. Her pulse was still skyrocketing, and as she worriedly licked her lips, she scanned her eyes slowly over the premises—first over the interior of the reception area, the neat desk, the muted carpet, the shelves lined with wedding-planning books. And then she looked through the windows. On one, the words Big Apple Brides were painted in gold. Draped with satin swags, both glassed cases brimmed with wedding items: champagne glasses, a hope chest, garters and bouquets. A winged mannequin wore a gown of white feathers, a bed waited in invitation, and roses were strewn across the floors. The effect was pure fantasy, inviting couples to come inside the shop and create their ultimate dreams.

There! Her heart beat double time. Yes…she recognized the man who was walking past now! She'd seen him more than once this morning. It wasn't her imagination. He didn't look dangerous, though. In fact, he was the picture of respectability, wearing a dark gray wool coat open over a light gray suit. His hair was short. Now he passed the window again, as if trying to decide whether or not to come inside.

A walk-in? Yes, she thought with sudden relief. That was probably the case. Ten to one, he was considering proposing to his girlfriend. After Stacy and Reggie were gone, he'd probably come inside to get estimates for a wedding. While paying for the event was the bride's family's responsibility, traditionally, the escalating cost of creating a perfect day was prompting more grooms to pitch in, sometimes even bearing the whole cost.

Good. Edie was so desperate for clients that she suddenly felt tears pushing at her eyelids. Not that she'd cry. Still, she simply couldn't stand one more thing in her life going wrong. And since starting Big Apple Brides had been her life dream, she really wanted it to fly. If the guy didn't return, Edie decided, she'd call Pete Shriver, just to make sure he hadn't put another security man on detail outside her shop without telling her.

What a day! *Months*, she mentally amended. Ever since she'd been hired to plan the Darden wedding, her life had spun increasingly out of control. The latest challenge was that her assistant, Cheryl, had quit. In itself, this would have been upsetting, but Cheryl's reason for leaving made things much worse. She'd run off with a man she'd met at Big Apple Brides—a man who'd come into the shop with his fiancé to plan their wedding. Now Cheryl was vacationing with him in St. Martin.

Unbelievable, Edie thought, suddenly fuming. Even worse, the stack of résumés faxed to her by a headhunter had hardly turned up the perfect replacement. Besides, Edie couldn't pay enough to attract the sort of assistant she really wanted. Before hiring the headhunter to screen applicants, most people who'd responded to her newspaper ad had shown up with tattoos and visible piercings. One had brought her dog. Another was addicted to chewing grape gum and was furious when Edie had told her she couldn't read novels on the job.

The man outside had vanished, so Edie turned her attention back to Stacy, who was saying, "Oh, Reggie, look, here's the list of songs Julia Darden's playing. I really do like her dress. I think I'd like to have one just exactly like it. What do you think, hon?"

"Please," Edie managed, still feeling caught between

a rock and a hard place. "We're going to have to move out of the conference room—"

"But we're hiring you because you're planning the Darden wedding," persisted Stacy.

"Of course," Edie agreed, glad for the business, "but I want to help you consider all the possibilities for your own wedding. So, if we could…"

Just as Stacy replaced the drawing of Julia's dress, a male voice sounded from behind Edie. "The dress really is stunning."

Edie turned, and when she saw the man framed in the door, she felt as if her whole world was sliding off-kilter again. It was the guy who'd been lurking outside. He breezed past Edie, heading for Stacy with a proprietary air as if he owned the place, and Edie wondered what was going on. Was he an acquaintance of Stacy and Reggie's? Had he been waiting for them? He was even better looking up close. Medium height, medium build, brown hair, brown eyes. A small mole by his mouth. Nothing special, but the whole package was appealing. So was the whiff of cologne he left in his wake.

Edie's jaw slackened as she watched him shrug out of a silk-lined coat that seemed to float down the arms of his snazzy suit. He clapped Reggie hard on the shoulder, then thrust out his hand, offering a quick, rough handshake. "Name's Seth Bishop."

Which meant he didn't know Stacy and Reggie, after all.

Nevertheless, he slid his hand under Stacy's elbow as if they'd known each other for years, then began steering her gracefully from the room, staring down at her from the vantage point of comparable height and sending her an utterly disarming, charming grin that clearly mesmerized the woman. As he passed Edie, he winked, and while she was still gaping, he took advantage of her stupefaction to deposit his coat into her arms.

"Thanks," she managed.

"No, thank you," he said, guiding Stacy across the threshold and into the next room, where Edie had been trying to direct her for the past ten minutes. As Edie and Reggie followed, the man calling himself Seth Bishop said, "That dress is great, but Julia Darden's one of those tall, skinny, willowy types…"

Stacy, who'd looked as if she'd been placed under a spell a second ago, now glanced over her shoulder at Edie, frowning. "Are you saying I'm not—"

"Scrawny?" He laughed. "Absolutely not." Turning, he winked at Reggie. "Julia's beautiful, yes. But in a sort of supermodel way. She's got a figure that needs to be fleshed out a bit, which is why Ms. Benning helped her choose the Empire gown you were admiring. You, however—" he glanced from Stacy to Reggie for support "—have other…" He paused delicately, as if searching for a word, then settled on, "Assets. And so, I think Ms. Benning intends to show you gowns that Julia Darden couldn't have gotten away with wearing…gowns that can show off your figure, and—"

"You're saying you think my figure's better than Julia Darden's?" Stacy asked breathlessly, chuckling with delight.

"Well," conceded Seth Bishop. "We don't like to compare clients."

The man was acting as if he worked here! Unsure whether she should be furious or relieved, Edie decided it was in her best interests to simply hang up the man's coat and start hauling down books of dress-design illustrations. The next hour passed in a blur. Seth Bishop, whoever he was, was a real hard-sell animal. He appealed to the couple's vanity and their pocketbook, but his methods hardly mattered because by the end of the hour, Stacy and Reggie were well on their way to creating their own dream wedding, rather than copying Julia Darden's.

Edie and this stranger had worked together beautifully, too, hand in glove. After setting Stacy and Reggie up with a future appointment, the man even showed the couple to the door, and when he shut it behind them and turned around to face her, Edie found herself laughing, dryly saying, "Should I be impressed or terrified?"

He raised a thick, dark eyebrow, his lips upturning in a warm, inviting smile, his dark eyes sparkling. "Terrified? Of me?"

Leaning against the desk behind her, Edie crossed her arms, surveying him a long moment. Unable to wipe the smile from her face, she felt strangely glad this was one of the mornings she'd gotten up early to wash and blow-dry her shoulder-length blond hair. She was wearing one of her most flattering suits, too, with a tailored A-line skirt and a dark brown forties styled jacket. She nodded. "Yeah, terrified. And resentful," she added.

He chuckled, his brows knitting in an expression of mock concentration, as if he had absolutely no idea what she was talking about. "Of *moi?*"

"I'd been trying to get Stacy out of the conference room for ten minutes when you got here."

"True. I was standing outside watching. But in your defense, she was a tough case. It seemed better to use guy charm."

Edie nodded. "Hmm. Guy charm?"

"My specialty."

From what she'd seen, she wouldn't disagree with him. "And you are?"

His mouth curled further, twisting into one of the most disarming smiles she'd ever seen. "Besides charming?"

"The charm piqued my interest," Edie assured. "Now I need more information." She paused. "I did see you outside, and I thought maybe…"

"Yes?"

"You wanted an estimate or something." Up close, it seemed obvious that the guy couldn't be connected to the Darden's security problems. Oh, Edie had seen enough movies to know that even serial killers could fool people. But she didn't really believe that. No, she trusted her own gut instincts about people, and this guy exuded basic decency. More than Edie had ever sensed upon meeting someone new, in fact. Everything about him—the way he carried himself, the tasteful way he was dressed, the depth of warmth in his dark brown eyes, his easy sense of humor—made her sure he was trustworthy. He did, however, look puzzled.

"Estimate?"

She nodded. "For a wedding."

A brief pause ensued, during which his luscious eyes widened, then he suddenly burst out laughing. "You thought I was getting *married*?"

Edie hardly wanted to examine her motives, but the truth was, she'd never been so instantly attracted to a man in her life as she was to Seth Bishop. One look— and she'd started imagining how he'd look with his clothes off. If the truth be told, she'd been through a dry spell. The last man she'd dated had wound up with her sister, so she was due some excitement. She considered. "Marriage," she repeated. "Is that such a strange idea?"

"Uh…yeah," he deadpanned as if he'd never heard of anything so ludicrous. "Especially since I don't even have a girlfriend."

Edie tried not to overreact to the information she'd been fishing for, but her chest got tight. "Then what are you…"

He looked surprised once more, then blinked as if he'd just come to his senses and swiftly slid a palm against his shirt, into the side pocket of the suit and withdrew a folded paper, which he handed to her. "Sorry. I thought the agency told you I was coming."

"Oh," she managed as she studied what turned out to be his résumé, barely able to believe it. "You're applying for the assistant's job?"

"I guess we had a kind of action-oriented interview."

As she scanned the résumé, she couldn't believe her luck. He was from Ohio, and in addition to graduating from art school, he'd worked as an art director at two high-profile companies. He also had experience in sales, which, given his handling of Stacy and Reggie, was pretty obvious.

"I won't lie," he said quickly. "I lost my last job in a company reorganization. There were no hard feelings, and I got a good severance. So, I am interviewing for more professional positions, in keeping with my background."

"And you're interested in Big Apple Brides because…"

"I want to hold out for a dream job, so I don't expect it to materialize overnight. I figured while I interview for something more permanent, it wouldn't hurt to keep a hand in, do some lighter work. The agency thought some of my skills might be of interest to you…."

It was almost too good to be true. Right now, all Edie really needed was support staff while she finished the Darden wedding. Then she'd have more breathing space. Not to mention more money, to hire the sort of permanent assistant she most wanted. She eyed Seth Bishop again. Pete Shriver had talked to the headhunting agency at some length, regarding how background checks were to be conducted, since employees would necessarily come into contact with Julia Darden. Also, Edie was to fax Pete the résumés of any applicants she hired, so she wasn't too worried about Seth Bishop in that respect.... "I know the agency checked your references," she said anyway, "but I'll need to do so again."

"Of course."

He didn't look the least bit nervous, which was a good sign. "If what you did here over the last hour is indicative of how you work, we should get along famously," she found herself saying.

"Then why don't you check my references and call me. I'm ready to start whenever you want me to come in."

"Deal." Edie stuck out her hand, and when his found hers, she was hardly surprised to feel heat flood her system. Nothing more than the casual touch made her every last nerve dance. And her last thought as he shrugged into his coat and walked through the door and into the swirling snow was that she would never be able to work with him without taking him upstairs to her apartment—and to bed.

"Stacy was definitely right about one thing," Seth said several days later as he helped Edie sort through the sketches on the board table. "That really is a beautiful gown. You and your mother did a great job."

Edie couldn't help but lean closer to him, drawn by the scent of his cologne and animal magnetism she simply couldn't resist. "Actually—" Deciding to take a break, she pulled out a chair, seated herself at the table, then looked at the picture again. "That was my own dream gown."

Following suit, Seth rolled a chair across the gray carpet and sat next to her. "Yours?"

Nodding, she took a deep breath, relaxing. "Thank you for everything," she inserted, instead of pursuing the conversation. It was their third day on the job together, and Seth really had turned out to be a godsend. Sexy, too. He'd done nothing to diminish the initial sense that she'd like to get into bed with him. Today, he was wearing a dark charcoal suit, blue shirt and an unlikely lime-and-red-striped tie that looked so fabulous it prompted her to say, "You do have an amazing eye for color, Seth." She'd met few people who could mix and match color and fabric with his unique flair. "Are you sure you want to go back into art directing?"

He laughed. "Offering to make me a partner?"

"Maybe," Edie teased. "You can go, by the way. It's about five. I've got to stick around for the mailman. I'm his last stop, and he brings in the papers, which should be in the outside box by now."

Seth made no move to leave, but merely surveyed her, an easy smile still on his lips. "You're evading the subject."

"Which was?"

He pointed at a sketch. "The gown."

She shrugged, blowing out a wistful sigh. "Honestly, a lot of Julia's wedding includes elements I used to fantasize about when I was a kid. Things I thought I'd have in my own wedding. Even the music. My sister Bridget's fiancé, Dermott, finally agreed to arrange some pieces. And I'd always thought of asking him, myself."

As if sensing the conversation was headed for deeper turf, Seth rose, circled around to a counter and poured them both cups of coffee, fixing hers with cream and sugar, the way she liked it, then he returned, setting hers down before reseating himself. "Why didn't you save the ideas for your own wedding?"

She considered. "You mean, besides the fact that I don't have over a million dollars to spend?"

"Yeah."

"And besides the fact that I've just about given up on ever having a wedding?"

He stared at her. "You can't be serious."

She thought a moment, then flashed him a smile, deciding to come clean with the whole story. "Maybe I should tell you the real reason I opened Big Apple Brides. You see, rumor has it that a Southern belle named Miss Marissa Jennings put a curse on all the Benning women during the Civil War when her own love life didn't work out," Edie began, then she plunged into the wealth of family stories told since time immemorial about the wedding curse, including the fact that Joe Benning wasn't her biological father, since her mother had previously been married to a man named Jasper Hartley.

"You don't remember him at all?"

She shook her head. "Nope. I was too little when he died. Bridget had just been born. And Mom met Joe shortly afterward, so he's all I've ever known as a father. It's been great. Our only real legacy from Jasper Hartley is the family's wedding curse."

"And because of this, no Benning woman will ever marry?"

"So the stories go."

"Not very nice of Miss Marissa," Seth commented, clearly warming to the tale. He leaned forward as if to hear better, coming so close that their knees touched under the table. He pulled away, but not before a white-hot jolt shot through Edie's system.

"No, it wasn't," she agreed. "Anyway, there are plenty of family stories about the ghost of Miss Marissa, so from an early age, I thought opening a wedding-planning business might…"

"Bring the Benning women better marriage Karma?"

She sipped her coffee, then made a show of smacking her lips, tilting the cup and toasting him since it tasted absolutely perfect. "Exactly."

Seth squinted. "But I met your sisters. Marley and Bridget, right? They've both stopped in. I thought the two of them said they were engaged."

Edie grinned. "See. My plan worked."

"Touché."

Her smile tempered as she glanced across the threshold and to the outer windows where twilight was waning and the snow was still falling. Her business was situated on the corner of Hudson and Perry streets and her parents, Viv and Joe, lived at the other end of the block. She had a sudden urge to call her mother, to ask if she could bring Seth Bishop home with her for dinner—assuming he'd want to come, of course. Her grandmother, fondly known as Granny Ginny, was still visiting, and she imagined Seth would enjoy the older woman's company.

Turning her attention to him again, she startled. He'd

been looking at her with…intensity, she realized. Longing. Raw sexual need. For just a second, she felt completely unbalanced, although she shared the sentiment, she was deeply attracted to him, and more than once she'd fantasized about going to bed with him. It was unwise, since they were working together, yes. Still, the more she got to know him, the more she wanted him. She also realized his knee had found hers under the table again. How long had it been brushing hers?

"Uh…" Somehow, she found her voice. "My sisters are engaged, but they've only became so recently." Continuing, now speaking almost by rote, since his proximity was claiming most of her attention, she caught Seth up on how her life had spun out of control after Sparky Darden had hired her. She told him about how *Celebrity Weddings* had talked her into going on a reality show called *Rate the Dates* with a man she'd been dating at the time, named Cash Champagne, and how he'd only been using her to get close to Julia Darden, since he was Sparky Darden's estranged biological son and Julia's half brother.

"That's a wild story," Seth agreed.

"Nothing compared to what happened after that," assured Edie, reporting that things had gone further awry since Marley, while attempting to cancel Edie's appearance on the reality show, had wound up being a contestant, herself—something that had led to her engagement with Cash. And then Bridget, determined to put an end to Miss Marissa's wedding curse on the Benning women for good, had talked her longtime best friend, Dermott, into traveling down South to an old family plantation in Florida, owned by their grandmother, to do some ghost-busting.

"According to Bridget, she rid the plantation of Miss Marissa, not to mention her curse, which is how Bridget wound up engaged to Dermott."

"Again, impressive," said Seth.

"And why I know no more adventures can come my way until after the Darden wedding," Edie finished, chuckling softly.

"I'm not sure I follow. Why?"

"I've had my quota," she explained.

He was smiling. "Well, you don't seem cursed to me."

"Believe me, my own luck's been lousy."

"You found me."

"True. But only after the videographer for the reality show I mentioned found out Marley had taken my place." She paused, suddenly pondering the wisdom of going into all this with a man to whom she was so attracted. "I hate to admit this, but they…they, uh, announced on national television that my love life was in the toilet."

His shoulders shook with merriment. "You're kidding me, right?"

She slowly moved her head from side to side. "I wish."

"Tell all."

She plunged into the story of how the videographer, a man named Vinny Marcel, had exposed that Marley was pretending to be her twin on the show. "Marley won, and I did get a cut of the money," she said, finishing, "and I put it into the business. Still, the publicity really wasn't good. I probably gained as many clients as I lost. And I lost some couples when Cheryl ran off with one of our customers, too."

"I promise I won't abscond with a bride," Seth offered.

"I'd appreciate it," said Edie. "I know it's tough on you. I could see you eyeing Stacy."

"Oh, please."

She laughed.

"Seriously. Did you really use ideas for your own dream wedding while planning Julia Darden's?"

She glanced over the sketches and photographs on the table. "Sure. This wedding could make or break my reputation, so I've wanted it to be perfect. And like most little girls, I always had a fantasy about what the ultimate wedding would be like."

"You do have great taste."

Edie looked at the picture of the dress, her heart suddenly aching. Seth was the only one who knew it had been her own dream outfit, and now unexpectedly, she almost wished she hadn't shared the design with the heiress, although she did like sharing her thoughts and emotions about the matter with Seth. Once more, her eyes drifted over him, and her internal thermometer climbed like a fever. She sighed. "Julia came to the table with so few of her own ideas," she admitted as she surveyed the dress for the thousandth time, admiring a square neckline calculated to show off an ample swell of breasts. Long sleeved, it was made of gossamer fabric, hand sewn with pearls and white crystals. "My mother helped with my initial vision of the design," she added. "And as I told you before, she's actually making it."

"She's good. If anyone I know ever needs a dress designer, I'll mention her."

"She'd love to hear you say it."

"And the ring?" he prompted.

"Bridget designed it. Here are the others." From under a stack of papers, Edie lifted out Bridget's discarded designs, letting Seth leaf through them.

Suddenly, he stopped and said, "This."

Edie could merely shake her head. At least once an hour, she found herself wondering if she'd met her soul mate. For the past three days, she'd barely dared to think it, and yet, their tastes and attitudes seemed impossibly in sync. She eyed the star-shaped setting of diamonds. "That's the ring I imagined for myself," she admitted. "And see—" She lifted another drawing. "The flowers are interwoven with lavender glass beads. Lavender's both my and Julia's favorite color, as it turned out. My dad, who works as a caterer, is making the cake. It's—" finding another picture, she put it before him "—this."

"Yum," Seth offered, taking in the four-tiered confection.

"Well," Edie conceded, her voice hitching with excitement. "You can do more with cakes. I even saw one recently that looked as if it was made of leather, but I really want this wedding to be almost all white. The tablecloths are white. The tents, just in case the weather warms up and we can move outside. I really hope it materializes the way I've imagined it. If so, it should be traditional, classy, beautiful."

"I'll do whatever I can to help."

"There's a matching bracelet that's attached to the ring by a thin chain," she found herself continuing. "It's only to be worn for fancy events. Like the wedding. Or maybe parties Julia attends in the future. And the necklace was to be—" rummaging, Edie found yet another drawing "—this simple long strand of diamonds that loops once around her neck."

"Wow."

Edie shrugged. "Julia chose another ring, but she's wearing the necklace. Still, she's pretty ambivalent."

Seth shook his head, as if to say that was a shame.

"She would have been happy with no ring at all," Edie said in her defense. "Julia's a simple person, really. She's madly in love, and just wants to settle down and start a family with as little fanfare as possible."

"So why the…"

"Expensive, beautiful three-ring circus?" Edie finished. "Her father pushed for it. Still, I think once all is said and done, Julia will be happy she and Lorenzo have the memories."

When she glanced up, her eyes locked with Seth's. This time, he didn't look away, and Edie simply couldn't. Her lips parted as if in anticipation, and she drew in a quick, audible breath. Simultaneously, she was aware Seth Bishop had registered her response. No doubt, he could guess that her heart was hammering again. Maybe he saw the pulse that was ticking too fast in her throat. Or felt the sudden jerk of her knee against his. And while he couldn't feel the heat pooling in her belly, or the sudden swift pang at her feminine core, maybe he could guess at it.

"What about your memories, Edie," he murmured.

Vaguely, she wondered if this was really happening. One moment, she'd been discussing Julia's wedding with her new assistant, and the next…

"My memories?" she managed.

"Definitely," he said, "I don't think you should give up on having a wedding for yourself that's every bit as beautiful."

Given the way he was looking at her, she almost felt as if he was proposing. It should have been unsettling, and yet such quick intimacy coming from this man, wasn't. With every passing minute, he seemed more like her perfect match. They were both morning people. Meat-and-potatoes people. Headache rather than stomachache people. And they both liked imported beer and fine wines. They took their coffee exactly the same way, and had read most of the same books. Most importantly, when it came to talking about weddings—colors, fabrics, music, meals—Edie had finally met someone with whom she could really talk shop. They were both on the same wavelength, and during conversations, they nearly stumbled over themselves, each trying to get words out first.

What about your memories, Edie? Had Seth Bishop really just said that? Feeling as if she was in a daze, Edie considered Bridget's ghost-busting trip once more. Had her sister really ended the wedding curse that had haunted the Benning women for years? Was it Edie's turn to find love now?

It seemed so crazy. But why? Every woman had to meet her true love somewhere. Why shouldn't this be Edie's moment? Why shouldn't this dark, snowy evening be The One? Her chest feeling tight, Edie leaned forward, wondering how he'd respond if she just pressed her lips to his....

She had a sudden urge—apropos of nothing—to just ask him to sleep with her. It was a risk, yes. But not knowing how Seth Bishop's flesh would feel pressed to hers seemed like a risk, also. She imagined herself saying something like, "We're both attracted, so do you want to skip all the usual preliminaries and come home with me?" The thought made her smile.

And then, over one of his shoulders, she saw the mailman at the door. "Oh—" she gasped, feeling suddenly flustered. "The mail. The papers. I forgot."

He leaned away, looking as affected as she at what might have been a near kiss, then he pursed his lips as if suppressing a full-fledged grin, his eyes dancing with awareness. "Good," he deadpanned. "For the last few minutes I've done nothing but wonder what was happening in the world at large."

Clearly, that had been the least thing on his mind. "Me, too," she agreed. Laughing, she playfully swatted him as she stood, swinging her hips more than necessary as she headed for the front door to meet the postman.

"Here's two packages you need to sign for," he said. "And all today's papers." After she'd signed, she took the parcels inside, set them on the reception desk, then looked at the front page of the *Post* and groaned. "Great," she muttered. At least the subject matter wasn't Julia. But maybe this was worse. Lorenzo Santini was buck naked in a locker room, and pretty well hung, Edie thought, judging by the size of the soft-focus fuzzy area meant to mask his private parts. He was deeply engaged in conversation with a woman other than his fiancée, and the headline said Darden Wedding Called Off? Why hadn't Pete Shriver called to let Edie know?

"I really can't believe this," she murmured, distracted when Seth sidled behind her. Nothing more than feeling Seth's chest brushing her back, the scent of his cologne and his breath on her neck was enough to make her forget the Darden wedding entirely, even though it had been her sole obsession for months. Seth really was just too good to be true. When Pete Shriver checked his references, he'd done so to protect the interests of his own client, Julia, but Edie was benefitting, also. How many women had a top-notch professional check out a potential boyfriend, after all?

More than potential, Edie decided as she turned toward Seth. He was close enough that she was nearly in his arms. The air between them spiked with raw heat.

"You know how I told you about Vinny Marcel?" she said, turning the *Post* so that Seth could see the photograph and headline. "The videographer from *Rate the Dates* who exposed how Marley took my place on the show?" she clarified.

He nodded. "Yeah."

"Well, I mention Vinny because there's only one person I hate more than Vinny, for making my life a living hell."

"And he is?"

"A guy named Jimmy Delaney."

Suddenly, his sexy dark-eyed gaze seemed so intense that Edie felt as if the air had just been sucked from the room. "You've heard of him." Angling his head, he leaned closer and for a second, she was sure he was going to kiss her now. Instead of answering, he said huskily, "Why don't we talk about all this over dinner? I'm starved."

Slowly, she licked her lips, staring into eyes that were but a hand's breadth away. "Sure. I'm starved, too." *For you*, she added silently, suddenly thinking she might really proposition him tonight.

3

"I HEAR WHAT YOU'RE SAYING," Seth began after they'd crossed Hudson Street and had claimed a back booth at a place called Hunan Pan, ordering a sampler platter that included various Chinese dishes they could share. "But—" he turned the newspaper around on the table-top, so she could look at it again "—Jimmy Delaney wasn't the photographer."

Surprised, Edie edged the paper toward the flickering flame from a candle on the table and squinted, so she could see in the dim light of the restaurant. "He wasn't?"

"No. It was some guy named Jack Stevens."

"Really?" Edie could barely believe it, but when she ducked her head and peered more closely, to read the byline, she saw Seth was right. She shook her head. "Most pictures of this sort have been taken by Jimmy Delaney," she murmured. Glancing up, she caught Seth's gaze. "He's a freelancer," she continued, explaining. "A member of the paparazzi. Pete Shriver—he's head of the Darden security staff—has been instrumental in getting eleven orders of protection against him. For some reason, Jimmy's really into shooting pictures of Julia."

"She is photogenic," Seth offered. "And I've seen

enough pictures of her that Jimmy Delaney can't be the only guy taking them."

"True. But *Celebrity Weddings* has exclusive rights to shoot the wedding preparations, as well as the event at the estate, and Jimmy goes out of his way to show up where he's not wanted."

"You're on a first-name basis," quipped Seth. "The sure sign he's a real archenemy."

"We're terrified he'll ruin the wedding."

Seth looked genuinely surprised. "Ruin the wedding? By trying to take pictures?"

She nodded. "He hardly has Julia and Lorenzo's best interests at heart."

"I doubt he wishes them ill."

"Maybe not."

"And people like this kind of picture," Seth argued.

She studied him a long moment. "Lorenzo's goodlooking," she admitted. "I'll give you that. And people are interested in following Julia's life, mostly because she's the epitome of class—wealthy, beautiful and also a genuinely nice person. But a picture such as this is calculated to harm her relationship with her fiancé."

"The headline maybe, but not the picture itself," Seth countered, playing devil's advocate. "Without the text, you'd just see a guy in the buff in a locker room with an unidentified woman."

Her jaw slackened. "I can't believe you're saying this, Seth! You're actually defending the photographer! The person who took this picture—" She looked down at the paper again, reading. "Jack Stevens," she repeated. "He knew exactly what the *Post* would do with such a picture. He knew how it would be used."

"Mere conjecture."

"You've been hanging around too long with your best friend," she scoffed, a smile lifting her lips abruptly, since Seth was obviously trying to rile her. He'd told her his best buddy from Ohio had become a lawyer and that they were still close. Seth was even playing uncle to the kids, which had further piqued Edie's interest. Her own family was tightly knit, and Seth's involvement with kids showed he might share her values, as had the way he'd spoken about his parents when the subject had come up. She suppressed a shiver that, coupled with her intense sexual attraction, could make for quite the combination.

"Well, you can't know what was going on in Jack Stevens's mind when he took the picture," Seth pointed out.

"And I don't want to," she shot back.

Smiling, he clucked his tongue. "What venom! And for people you don't even know."

"And don't want to," she repeated, her lips curling.

Lowering his chin, he sent her a long look from under heavily lidded eyes. "Are you really saying you've never been sucked into staring at a lurid tabloid headline with curiosity? That you've never stopped in your tracks in the street near a news kiosk, just to look at the headlines?"

Crossing her arms, she leaned back in the booth, narrowed her gaze and glared at him playfully. After a long pause, she assured, "Never."

"Hmm. Never watched *Entertainment Tonight*?"

She squinted. "You're trying to make which point?"

"That if you didn't contribute by becoming part of the market for pictures such as this, the paparazzi would cease to exist. If no one looked, photographers would be out of business. You could cancel your subscription to the *Post*, you know." He paused. "Now, tell me you've never once bought *People* magazine."

Even she could feel the guilty flush creeping into her cheeks. "Not even once," she lied.

"I don't believe you."

"Whose side are you on, anyway?"

"I didn't know I had to choose."

"Playing both sides of the fence?"

"Always."

"You must be a Gemini."

"Guess again."

"Leo."

"Why's that?"

"You've got a lot of outward charm."

"Thanks. And you were warm. It's my rising sign."

"Ah. Virgo," she guessed again. "Into control."

"Nope. Scorpio. In three planets."

"Dangerous."

"Sexy. You?"

He was asking for her sun sign, but she only laughed. "Ditto. Very sexy. So I've been told."

"Let me say it to you again then. Sexy."

"Less so if you're a two-timer," she retorted. "Around me, you need to choose sides."

"If you insist."

"Okay. So once more, whose side are you on?"

"The one that gets you the most agitated."

Or aroused.

She was enjoying the banter more than anything in a long time. The past months had been hectic and stressful, but shooting the breeze with Seth made her feel as if weights were being lifted from her shoulders. "You like annoying me?"

His dark eyes were sparkling now, catching the light of the candle. Reaching, he used a forefinger to brush away a lock of hair from her forehead. "Sure do."

Suddenly, she felt breathless. "Mind telling me why?"

The finger settled on her temple for a split second, then trailed down her cheek before he playfully tapped the tip of her nose and released another low, throaty chuckle. "Because your skin gets flushed," he began, his voice lowering a husky notch, "and I can see your pulse quickening, and I imagine your heart beating wildly, and your eyes starting to flash fire...."

She couldn't help but burst out laughing. Usually, seeing a picture such as that in the *Post* would ruin her day, but tonight, sitting here flirting with Seth Bishop, it hardly seemed to matter. "You have a way with words. I take it I've discovered yet another of your talents, Seth."

"Beyond?"

"Mixing and matching fabrics."

He rolled his eyes, then bit down on his lower lip with two perfectly straight, gleaming white teeth. "Oh, Edie," he returned, his eyes locking into hers, "I've got plenty of talents beyond what you've seen me do in your conference room."

"You do make a perfect cup of coffee."

"And so much more."

She was still imagining what such a comment could mean when a waiter appeared, placing the sampler platter between them, and setting down two plates. Once the man had gone, Seth unwrapped paper from around his chopsticks, then expertly situated them between his fingers, lifted a piece of chicken and held it out, in front of Edie's lips. So, he was going to feed her now? she thought, feeling a rush of excitement. For the past three days, her life had certainly started to get interesting, and she was glad that she'd opted for the restaurant, instead of taking him to her parents' apartment. With her folks and Granny Ginny around, she'd never have an opportunity to get to know Seth. Who knew where this could lead?

"The food looks excellent," he said.

"Because both my parents and I live on this street, we wind up eating here a lot. It's always good." Coming closer, she parted her lips and took the bite, feeling juicy tender meat explode inside her mouth. "It's not the first time I'm glad I didn't go the vegan route like my sister Marley," she announced after she'd swallowed.

He winced, shooting her a sympathetic glance. "A vegan?"

"Only food. She hasn't started wearing the shoes."

He looked skeptical. "Shoes?"

"Haven't you heard of that place called Moo Shoe in the East Village?"

"Nope."

"Pleather goods."

"Gotcha."

Edie shrugged as he used the chopsticks to further fish around the platter, her throat tightening as his knee suddenly knocked hers under the table. It instantly corrected itself, pulled away, changed its mind, then found hers again, this time pressuring firmly. He had nice knees, too. Big and hard. More square than rounded. Even though there was nothing in her mouth at the moment, Edie swallowed, hard. Once more, she had a strong urge to simply proposition him. But how? She imagined herself just saying, "Do you want to go to bed." But that sounded so, well, crass. Still, given the energy coursing between them, she didn't think he'd be surprised. She was sure he'd say yes, too. "Well," she amended. "After Marley's divorce—she was married once—she fell off the wagon and started eating at McDonald's."

"Falling off the wagon usually pertains to drinking," he said.

"Uh...Marley did some of that, too. Nothing dangerous," she clarified, laughing. "Wine nights with the girls."

"I take it you were one of the girls?"

She nodded. "Sure. But only because I was playing Good Samaritan, trying to help her get on her feet after the divorce."

"Ah. Kind enough to drink fine Burgundy for a cause."

"Of course. I'm the good twin."

He didn't look convinced. His eyes were saying that any woman as sexy as Edie probably wasn't going to continue being good for long. Nothing could be further from the truth. "Marley was always the wild child," she explained. "Boy crazy, wearing wild clothes, listening to loud music. Bridget's the youngest. I think she always felt a little left out, because Marley and I were so focused on each other." She shrugged, trying to turn her mind off the tingling sensation where their knees touched. "I guess I was always trying to show Marley up. Our relationship got pretty competitive when we were kids. So..."

"You dressed in button-down suits, read a lot and listened to classical music instead of rock and roll."

"That's about the size of it."

"Surely some guy came along to loosen you up."

She tried to mask her wistful expression, but couldn't. Seth Bishop's gaze was too probing, too perceptive, and his physical proximity was affecting her concentration. "Honestly?"

When he spoke, his voice had lost its playful edge, and it sounded smooth and soothing. "Yeah, honestly. I'd like to get to know you."

Her shoulders rose and fell, and she blew out a long suffering sigh. "Some came around. But because I was more prim and proper, the guys usually wound up going for Marley." Her smile broadened. "And well…you've met Marley."

He returned the smile. "Tight spandex workout pants, visible sports bra under mesh T-shirts."

"And there I was in my gray suits."

He rolled his eyes. "You look good in them, and you know it."

"Thanks. I was fishing for a compliment."

"I'm good at taking bait." He paused, his gaze suddenly dropping to the blouse she wore beneath her suit. "You know onlookers do get occasional glimpses of…uh, lace beneath."

She grinned. "Really? I had absolutely no idea."

"I'll bet."

"Regarding my uncheckered past," she continued, her cheeks warming with the knowledge that he'd noticed her lace lingerie. "I did manage to make much better grades than Marley in high school."

"Now that sounds fun."

"A blast," she assured.

"What about after high school?"

"Marley and I went to the same college. And my pattern of dateless nights continued."

He shot her a mock doleful expression. "And now?"

Now she was determined to break out of the box, and while she felt compelled to say so, Seth Bishop was her employee. Oh, they'd nearly kissed in the conference room at Big Apple Brides less than an hour ago, and she'd thought of taking him straight upstairs to her apartment, but she knew it wasn't wise to mix business and pleasure. She couldn't help but blurt out, "We work together, Seth. Uh…I'm enjoying myself, but maybe the flirtation's going a bit too far."

His eyes widened slightly. "Hmm…we've worked together for three days."

"Meaning?"

"I could quit."

That caught her off guard, and she guffawed. "You'd end your wedding-planner career just for me?"

His face was stone solemn. "Absolutely, Edie."

"Couples will be heartbroken."

"Not as much as me if you don't let me get to know you."

"You really are a charmer, you know."

Didn't he really mean sleep with her?

"I've been working on my techniques for years," he assured.

While she considered, he glanced down, as if only now realizing he'd ceased fishing on the platter with his chopsticks. Ponderously lifting broccoli and mushrooms, he finally settled on a piece of succulent beef that was dripping with Szechuan sauce. "Hmm. Here. While you're considering my future in the workforce, try another bite."

But she didn't want to sweep this under the rug. "I'm attracted to you," she admitted, thinking that was an understatement. "And so our working together complicates things...."

He merely eyed her. "Eat, Edie."

She didn't really want to. No, she wanted to air the emotions warring within her, and maybe share her bed with him. Instead, she bent closer, parted her lips once more, and suddenly, everything taking place seemed truly overwhelming—the salty taste in her mouth as he deposited the beef, his knee feeling hard against hers, his eyes smoldering as he watched her chew. "The food's great as usual...." she found herself saying.

"But?"

"I think I'm losing my appetite."

He frowned in concern. "Are you okay? You said you were a head person, not a stomach person—"

"Thanks for remembering."

"Did the stress of seeing the photograph get to you?"

"Yes. But that's not it. And when I called Pete Shriver he was adamant about leaving the worrying to him. We're not security specialists. Our job's to produce the most gorgeous wedding New York's ever seen."

"Must be tough to please a guy like Sparky Darden."

"He definitely knows quality work," she agreed. "Anyway, I guess I just..." She paused, then decided she should just spit it out. "Do you want to go to my place, Seth?" She paused, then raced in. "Like I said, I'm attracted to you. And, well, you seem attracted to me. And I just..."

"Wondered what it would be like to sleep with me?"

She blew out a shaky breath. "Yes."

After another second's thought, he said, "When?"

"Now? As in before we even eat?"

Certainly, getting up and leaving the restaurant in

midmeal was crazy. Nevertheless, he set down his chopsticks. And then he said, "Let's go."

"HOLD STILL," SAID MELISSA. "Before you go out, I want to take a picture of you for my class, okay? We're going to develop pictures next Saturday."

Predictably, both her parents looked relieved that she was taking such an interest in the photography class. "Honey, we're in a real rush," murmured her mother, Chynna. "Now, I want you to promise me you'll be nice to Mrs. Rodriguez."

"I will," vowed Melissa, who'd already eavesdropped as her parents filled the sitter in on their daughter's latest difficulties. Not that it mattered. As soon as her parents were gone, Mrs. Rodriguez, who was hard of hearing, always turned up the volume on the television and watched sitcoms. As far as she was concerned, Melissa was going to be doing homework in her room all evening, which meant Melissa could climb out the window, down the fire escape and have a business meeting with Jack. She was taking a series of pictures of him, too, which she hoped would impress Jimmy Delaney. On her and Jack's first sale alone, they'd made more than enough to cover a whole trip to a rehabilitation center.

"We'll be glad to pose, doll," her father, Tyrone, was saying. "But you'll have to make it snappy."

"Snappy," squealed Melissa, laughing. "I get it."

Her dad winked, and she winked back, causing his grin to broaden.

"Get close together," she crooned. Her parents snuggled in front of a picture window, and behind them, Melissa could see the sparkling city lights, and her heart tugged wistfully. Her mother was right. They really did have so much. They were blessed. From their high-rise in Harlem, they had a super view of the city, and even if they were never around, Melissa sometimes thought her parents loved her. Her mom was beautiful, too. Unlike Melissa, who was scrawny and gangly, and who wore her hair in a flip, her mom was tall and what people always called statuesque—a bit like Whitney Houston. She'd been a singer years ago, back when she was in her twenties—she was thirty-five now—and she'd cut one hit record. She'd met Melissa's daddy when he was traveling for the NFL, between seasons, because she'd sung the national anthem before a sporting event.

Melissa blew out a sigh, trying to hold the camera steady, thinking of the other kids in Jimmy Delaney's class. They'd come from different walks of life, but most were from the downtown area. Basically, they seemed a lot like her. Just kids who felt bored and who'd been looking for things to do in their spare time. A boy named Timmy had started using credit cards, just as Melissa had, to order rare comic books on eBay. And Josh corresponded online with an older woman in Texas for a year before she realized he was just a kid and too young to really be her boyfriend. He felt bad about it, too. He really hadn't meant to break her heart.

"Okay," Melissa said, "now kiss!"

Her parents laughed, snuggled closer, and although she spent much of her time being mad at them, Melissa felt a rush of pleasure at seeing them look so happy together. She snapped the shutter. "Super!" she enthused.

"Now, we've really got to run," her mother said.

And within a minute, they were out the door. They didn't even kiss Melissa goodbye.

4

"NICE PLACE," JIMMY DELANEY said as he watched Edie twisting the three locks on the door, sliding the dead bolts back into place.

"At the moment, my apartment's an extension of the shop, so I hope you'll forgive," quipped Edie, glancing over her shoulder and nodding toward boxes stacked in a corner. "Champagne glasses," she explained. "Plates. Silver. Place cards. Favors. All of it goes to the Darden estate this Sunday. My dad's driving the truck. We'll probably finalize the plans over dinner Friday night. I usually go to my folks then," she clarified. "So do my sisters."

She turned and leaned against the door. Even from here, he could see the pulse vibrating in her throat, and now he realized she was chattering because she was nervous. So was he. Especially since he was lying to her about his identity.

"I didn't want to clutter the shop with things that were more easily delivered in Manhattan," she continued, "and I didn't want smaller items going to the estate piecemeal. A lot of the items here are important, and I want to hand-carry them. This close to the wedding, I'd just die if something was lost or broken. Only the heavier things are being delivered to Long Island, such as the tents and chairs." Pausing breathlessly, she sighed. "I wish I could be in two places at once, but with Cheryl gone, and you new to the job..."

"Given the size of your business, the Darden wedding is..."

"Go ahead and say it," she agreed. "Too big for me. When I got the job, I'd just opened my doors and was spending most of my time phoning reception venues such as the Elks Club in Far Rockaway. However," she added, "I feel I've risen to the challenge. Who knew I'd be having meetings with celebrities and bodyguards?" She chuckled. "Did I tell you how I landed the wedding, Seth?"

Jimmy shook his head, half-glad for the small talk, and still wondering about Jack Stevens. Jimmy knew every celebrity photographer in the city, and he'd never even heard the name, nor seen the guy's pictures before today. The shot hadn't been bad, especially given the subject matter. Naked shoots were always difficult. Because of the low angle of the camera, Jimmy figured Jack Stevens must have been lying on his stomach somewhere in the locker room. But how had a grown man managed to escape detection? Why hadn't Lorenzo spotted him?

Jimmy blew out a breath, still studying Edie. Given the sexual energy coursing between them in the restaurant, he could barely believe they weren't already in bed. It was a good thing they weren't, too, he suddenly decided. Maybe he'd come to his senses and do what he should have days ago—walk out of Edie Benning's life.

Before, when he'd been seated in Judge Diana's courtroom, starting to come up with a plan about how to get pictures of the Darden wedding, inserting himself into Edie's life had seemed like a good option. Now, he wasn't so sure.

"No," he finally prompted, forcing his mind back to the conversation. "I don't think you mentioned how you got the job."

"I had made an infomercial," she explained, "advertising my new business, and while it's true Sparky Darden saw it on late-night television, what I didn't know until later was that he and my dad go way back."

"No kidding."

When she shook her head, hair that his fingers itched to touch swirled around her shoulders. "Dad worked in the kitchen of a hotel years ago, when Sparky was first getting his start."

"And he recognized you?"

"Yep. From my name. And he hired me, wanting to do a favor for my dad."

"Your dad must be quite a guy."

"That's an understatement. You'll have to meet him."

He hedged. "I'd love to." Although he knew the answer, he added conversationally, "The wedding's next Sunday?"

"Yeah." She sighed. "It's been the most hectic six months of my life, so I'll be glad when it's over. Still, I hope it's successful enough to bring in more high-profile clients. Right now, I've got a cash-flow problem. There's a lot of overhead. After the checks due to me arrive, and if I get new business on top of that, things should pick up. At least I hope so. I need to hire a larger staff, but I can't do it yet."

He frowned in concern. He'd hate to see Edie lose a venture she'd invested so much of herself in. "But if everything goes smoothly over the next few weeks, you should be in good shape, right?"

"Yeah."

"The exposure in *Celebrity Weddings* has got to help."

"Yes and no. I think it's been counteracted by my mention on *Rate the Dates*. That was a real setback. Because it looked as if my sister wound up with a man who'd been my boyfriend, we didn't exactly look like the sort of people who should be planning weddings. Besides, they'd talked about the Benning wedding curse on the show—they seemed to think it made for a good human interest story. And who wants to hire a wedding planner whose own love life is jinxed?"

"You don't really believe that about yourself, do you?"

She didn't look as if she really did. "Absolutely."

He let it pass. "Your folks aren't technically partners, though. I mean, it's not really a family business, right?"

"Not technically. But everybody's got skills that can contribute. Marley's been writing a series of articles for *Celebrity Weddings* called "Wedding Workouts," for instance, and she's Julia's personal trainer. After the wedding, she's going to take the money she won on *Rate the Dates* and re-open a fitness business she'd started once before called Fancy Abs. As near as I can tell, she and Cash are going to be a two-city couple. He owns a bar on Bourbon Street in New Orleans, and now there are some rumors that he may wind up doing some work for Sparky Darden's hotel business, as well. Anyway, like I mentioned before," she continued, circling back to the original subject. "Bridget designs rings, Mom sews and Dad cooks."

It was a lot to take in, yet the details didn't matter nearly as much as how Edie's blue eyes warmed when she spoke of her loved ones. "Nice family."

"It is." She flashed a smile. "They always say I'm a romantic at heart. I love working with my family. It's the best. Someday, I want one of my own."

Damn. Just looking at her, he felt his heart ache. The woman was golden. A real gem. Sweet. Kind. Loving. So, what the hell was he doing here? He glanced around the living room of her small one bedroom apartment, mentally kicking himself. Had he lost his mind? Usually, he thrived on disguising himself to get close to his photo subjects. He'd been doing it for the past few years, ever since he left the world of high fashion, art photography and art direction; usually doing so provided him with an adrenaline rush, but it wasn't happening tonight.

And he sure as hell didn't want to hurt Edie Benning. When he'd first seen her, he was calling himself Vinny Marcel and working as a videographer for *Rate the Dates*. He'd gotten an undeniable case of the hots for her, something that had only become increasingly acute over the past three days while he'd worked with her. But he'd learned quite a lot about her, too. Enough to know she was probably the nicest woman who'd ever shown an interest in him. A far cry from his usual partners. Not that he had anything against Tina from the Suds Bar, or Angel, who waited tables at the Avenue A deli, where he usually ate breakfast, but to say neither was looking for a real relationship would be an understatement.

He took a deep breath. Even without coming here, he could have drawn a picture of Edie's apartment, just from the images her personality had conjured in his mind. Everything was muted, soft and beautiful. The walls were painted such a light gray that to a less discerning eye, the color would have appeared white, and the moldings were done in nearly translucent peach; both colors were repeated in an old tapestried fabric rimmed with fringe that covered an old sofa. The sofa, itself, bespoke romance, with a high, carved back, rolled arms and fluffy, feather-filled cushions. Layers of white sheers hung, one behind the other, in the windows, so he could glimpse the snow flurries beyond, swirling under a glowing white moon. He shook his head. According to the news, there was a chance the temperature would hit the sixties again by the weekend.

Unpredictable, he thought. Just like whatever was happening between him and Edie.

"Most of the furniture's from secondhand shops," she admitted, interrupting his thoughts. "Marley and Bridget helped me paint. Mom made the curtains. She found the fabric covering the sofa somewhere down in Chinatown."

"Looks like a professional did the place."

She feigned offense. "I *am* a professional."

"If you ever get out of the wedding business, you could do interiors."

"My, my," she said, abruptly pushing away from the door and slowly walking toward him, "are you always so work obsessed?"

He felt anything but. In fact, his chest was squeezing tightly, as if heavy bands were wrapping around it with every step she took. As she sauntered closer, she shrugged out of the camel coat she'd been wearing, tossing it into a chair. He couldn't help but notice how the heels she wore accentuated the shapeliness of her calves, nor ignore how her stockings whispered, rustling against her skirt. His eyes settled where the hem raised above her knees, and then he glanced upward. Somehow, another of the top buttons of her silk blouse had come undone, and now, as she continued moving, he could see edges of lace peeking from under fabric he knew would feel like water. As heat flooded his groin and spread to his extremities, he realized he was already hard. He'd never touched her, never kissed her. But he'd been fantasizing for weeks....

And when she stopped in front of him, just a foot away, her blue eyes were appraising, as if she'd just realized she had the upper hand and was enjoying it. "Aren't you going to take off your coat?"

"Maybe I shouldn't," he found himself saying.

Disappointment crossed her features, and just seeing it made his heart tug, reminding him he actually had one. She was standing close enough now that he could draw her into his arms if he wanted to, close enough that he could smell the heady floral scent of her perfume. Almost against his will, he found himself inhaling deeply, just to draw it more deeply into his lungs.

"You changed your mind about wanting me?" she whispered huskily, her eyes daring him.

Never. How could any man not want Edie Benning? Every time he saw her, he felt like getting on his knees and begging. Which was exactly why he didn't want to hurt her. Glancing away, he blinked his eyes as if that would make him come to his senses. Maybe he was too far gone. One look at her—and everything in his life that had seemed solid only days ago now seemed flaky and ready to crumble.

His eyes found hers again. So did a finger he lifted to her face. He'd meant to press it against her lips, to indicate they should walk away and not even discuss what had almost happened between them, but when the finger brushed her lips, they held it like glue. A heartbeat later, she curled her fingers around his, drawing his hand down to her chest. As another button of her fell open, she slipped his hand inside her blouse without taking those hot blue eyes off his. He gasped, touching silk that put the fabric of the blouse to shame. She was hot there. Her skin flushed, warm and feverish. And as his fingers curled farther inside the cup of a bra, he found a nipple....

When she inhaled sharply, the sound shot to his groin. Seemingly encouraged, she kept her hand over his, coaxing him to explore her further—and against his better judgment, he did—rolling the taut tip between his thumb and forefinger, his own breath catching, his mouth growing dry. His voice was low and husky when he said, "Are you sure about this?"

She didn't speak, but her hand tightened over his, and although her head was tilted back, her half-shut eyes found his.

Her voice caught. "Why the second thoughts?"

He could hardly tell her who he really was. And because of that, he sure as hell couldn't make love to her. That his whole body was aching, crying out for her hardly mattered. Even worse, over the past three days, he felt he'd come as close as he ever would to finding a women he could describe as a soul mate. More than once, he'd had the thought that Edie Benning could be the love of his life. The One. It was probably untrue. He'd experienced the feelings, though. In his mind, he'd caught himself saying all the things he'd heard Ches say during the week when he'd met Elsa.

Well, maybe such things were academic at the moment. His hand was still on Edie's breast. The nipple was so tight and hot, that he had to feel it on his tongue. Somehow—hell if he knew how—her blouse had come all the way undone, and despite the crazy thoughts swirling through his mind, he knew he had to see just a little more skin before he stopped....

So, he flicked open the front catch of the bra. She was unbelievably full, succulently ripe. Petite, yes, and not large breasted, but she was beautiful. Slowly, his glazing eyes followed the sloping skin, while his hand traced the plump undercurve. Then he leaned, moaning softly, drawing in a sharp breath that sizzled between his clenched teeth during the second before he closed his mouth over where she ached for him. She tasted even better than she looked. Salty. Sweet. And in response, he suddenly braced himself, as if sensing he wouldn't be able to withstand the coming onslaught of pleasure, the muscles of his long legs tightening, his buttocks lifting, straining.

He had to stop. Already, she was too much. His mind had raced so far ahead of the game. He was imagining his flat palm rushing down her back, closing over her backside, lifting the hem of her skirt and finding the waistband of her panty hose. He wanted...inside. Leaning back a fraction, trying to force himself to put an end to the charade, he only wound up blowing hot breath on the wet rosy nipple he'd kissed. He loved the shudder that came in the wake, too. She was shaking with need.

Thrusting his tongue to catch a last droplet of her taste, he flicked it against the bud. Over and over, he vibrated the tip, until she was whimpering, releasing a series of barely audible, indecipherable sighs of need. He sensed her thighs moving, and he knew she was opening for him, parting her legs. The toes of her feet, still encased in the sexy, high-heeled shoes, were turning outward....

His heart was hammering hard. He could barely

catch his breath, and his mouth had gone so dry, that he was half tempted to excuse himself and get a drink of water. Not that he would. What he really needed was more of Edie Benning. To drink the fine wine of her body until his thirst was quenched. *Get out of here, Jimmy*, his mind screamed.

His erection was throbbing painfully against the zipper of his trousers as he inched away. Licking dry lips, he glanced into a face that had been transformed by what they'd just done. Her cheeks were flushed, pink and warm, and her blue eyes looked darker and almost thunderous, closer to the color violet.

Swallowing hard, Jimmy tried to catch his breath. And then he lifted both palms, gently cupping both her breasts, loving them with his hands—molding and shaping them a final, blissful moment. And then he did something so out of character that he could barely believe he was doing it. He rehooked the clasp of her bra, and carefully pulled together the silk sides of the blouse.

Struggling to clear his throat, he said, "We work together." It was a lame excuse, but then, she was the one who'd first mentioned that.

She considered a moment.

And then she nodded.

Just as he sighed with relief, she stepped forward. Before he could protest, she'd swiftly cupped a hand around the back of his neck and forcefully pulled his mouth to hers. The kiss erupted, shooting molten lava through his system. Both their mouths were open, wet. Her tongue thrust hard and he was gone, drowning in her…in what he knew they were about to become to each other. As she pushed the coat from his shoulders, he angled his head down, and as it hit the floor, his arms wrapped around her waist, hauling her closer. Jointly, they gasped when their lower bodies locked like their mouths.

Her teeth captured his lower lip, suddenly, and she lightly bit, her hands racing over his back now, gliding to his buttocks. These weren't the delicate, slender hands that Jimmy associated with Edie's lithe body, but hard, greedy hands that drew him even closer as her mouth slammed to his again, building damp heat and wet fire.

Without warning, she dropped to her knees. It happened so quickly that it took his fogged mind a moment to catch up. By then, her hands were wrestling with his belt, raking at it. She unsnapped the button of his slacks, her knuckles worrying his erection as she quickly jerked down the zipper. It was as if she couldn't get to him fast enough. "Damn," he muttered simply. "Damn."

He really had to get out of here. Yeah, he thought. He'd better come to his senses like a decent human being...the kind of decent man he hadn't been for years...the kind of man Edie Benning deserved. But how could he? She was pushing his trousers over his hips now. Damp shaking fingers hungrily dipped inside the waistband of his briefs, and then he went blind.

He wasn't even sure from what—pleasure? Pain? Lust? Relief flooded him when she ripped the cotton briefs to his thighs, trapping them instead of his engorged flesh, which was now thankfully released. The splayed fingers of one of his hands wound up in her hair. He'd meant to pull her upward, but the fingers only tightened in blond silken strands that spilled over his fingers looking like fresh-harvested wheat.

"Edie," he managed to say, his voice strained. He'd

never felt so powerless. "C'mon." *Maybe we better stop.* But he didn't say the words aloud because he'd sooner die than have her really heed them.

Especially when her mouth found him. The hand in her hair stilled. It simply froze on top of her head. For a moment, he was sure he'd never even be able to move again.

His eyes slammed shut, his hips thrust, and suddenly, his mind was no longer working at all. A mouth that could no longer form words slackened. The pleasure was beyond anything he'd ever experienced. Maybe it was because Edie was so sweet, so delicate, such a—as she liked to put it—good girl. Or maybe it was because everything had happened so fast, and the woman he'd wanted had come on him unexpectedly, like a sexual steamroller....

Either way, he was utterly lost. As her tongue swirled maddening circles around the head of his penis, sending his senses into overdrive and oblivion, he felt his eyes rolling back in his head. Vaguely, he thought he didn't want to come like this...not when it was their first time. He wanted to be deep inside her....

"Damn," he whispered once more. Didn't she know she was torturing him? Her liquid hot mouth seemed to squirt scalding heat down every inch of him as she slowly, deeply brought him inside, her lips sliding over each ridge....

"Ah...ah...ah..." One long unbroken groan split the air, and then he whispered, "Please, please, please," although he had no idea why, the words just a senseless pattering, his hands helplessly stroking the beautiful strands of her hair. She was amazing. So unbelievable. And he was going to burst....

Abruptly, he leaned away. Slowly, he kneeled in front

of her, and when they were eye level again, he angled his head, gently covering her mouth with his. The kiss was special. Very slow, hot and thorough. Barely able to catch his breath, he looked into her eyes and realized her blouse and bra were gone. She'd been undressing herself. Her skirt was unzipped. Reaching, he caught the hem and guided it upward, until he pulled it over her head. His heart hammered when he saw she wasn't wearing panty hose, after all, but only thigh-high stockings that held themselves up, without garters.

Which meant she was almost naked. Sliding a palm over the white tuft of silk panty covering her, he lost his ability to breathe once more. She wasn't just wet there. She was drenched. Gasping, he felt the moisture come off in his hand. And when he ducked his fingers beneath the waistband, his mind hazed. She was blond there, and the hairs were pure satin. "It's like touching air," he whispered.

"Romantic way of putting it," she whispered back.

"I'm the artsy type," he reminded.

"Draw me a picture."

"Sure." Keeping his eyes riveted to hers, so he could watch her pleasure build, he used a finger to part her cleft, carefully widening the slit, opening it all the way down until he found the place from which all that heat emanated. "First," he whispered huskily, "I'm going to draw a simple line."

His mouth found hers once more, his tongue gliding along the silk of her inner cheek as he pushed a finger inside. Her hips lifting instantly, arching, so she could take the pleasure. "Now, some circles," he whispered. Using a thumb that was now slick and warm, he flicked her clitoris, soliciting a sudden sharp cry.

"Do you like my picture?" he coaxed, sliding a hand around her back to better support her as she arched against him, his heart flooding with sensations he hadn't felt for years as she feathered kisses on his mouth.

"What are…are you drawing now…" she said, the words broken.

"The sun," he whispered, pressing his thumb to her clitoris, then rubbing ever deeper circles. "And the moon," he added hoarsely, pushing two fingers slowly, deeply inside her. "And the stars…"

She tightened then, arching to meet the thrust of his fingers a last time, her whole body shaking. As he felt her shuddering release, something primal came over him, and he urged her backward, onto the floor, his fingers still deep inside, the palpitations sending shocks through him. The look on her face was even more exciting to him than the response of her body.

Her eyes were wide, her mouth open. She was waiting. Even though she was coming, she still wanted more. So did he. Ever so slowly, he withdrew his fingers, and then he covered her whole body with his own, settling between her legs, aching to be inside…where his fingers had just been.

Propping his elbows on either side, he cupped her head with his hands, vaguely aware they'd be more comfortable in her bedroom, but hardly wanting to ruin the moment by suggesting they move. When he spoke, he barely recognized his own voice. It was so hoarse, it sounded as if he hadn't spoken for years. "Condoms?"

She merely arched again, her hips seeking his, her legs twining where his trailed on the floor. "I don't want one," she whispered simply.

He was stunned.

But he knew what to do. "Okay," he managed to whisper. He was hardly going to deny her request. It had been years since he'd felt a woman without any barrier. And this wasn't just any woman. It was Edie Benning. Taking a deep breath, he lifted his body away just for a second, and then, without otherwise moving, keeping his hands tucked protectively under her head and his eyes locked on hers, he let his heat find hers like a divining rod. He entered her slowly, sinking into her open warmth inch by inch, breath by breath.

And then they were gone.

5

"READY FOR ANOTHER HELPING of turkey, Seth?" Viv Benning asked a few evenings later, her eyes finding Jimmy's across a lace-covered table laden with platters from which steam rose, carrying scents of roasted meat and baked bread. Through the windows, slivers of the Hudson River were visible between buildings, and city lights gleamed in the rippling steely waters, seemingly flickering, igniting the sky's rose-tinged twilight just as the tapers inside the apartment lit the table's centerpiece of fresh spring daisies.

Jimmy startled, only belatedly remembering he'd been introduced as Seth Bishop. "No, but thank you," he managed to say to Viv Benning, guilt washing over him as he lifted a roll from a passing basket. He shouldn't be eating here, and he knew it, but ever since his mouth had found Edie's and he'd drowned in the first kiss, he'd been powerless to walk away. The game in which he'd involved himself would play out badly, though. Lying to your lovers always did. About that, Jimmy had no illusions. The truth, he thought now, will out. That's what his father had always said, but this was the first time in Jimmy's life he'd wished the old adage was wrong.

"Glad you came?" Edie whispered conversationally,

snuggling closer against his side, her face beaming. On her way to her parents', she'd said she was glad to have a date of her own tonight, since Marley and Bridget had been bringing their fiancés on Friday nights. Lately, Edie had felt like a fifth wheel.

"Are you kidding?" Jimmy returned. Reaching under the tablecloth, he slid a hand along Edie's thigh, then downward toward her knee, a rush of warmth coursing through him when his palm left the fabric of her teal skirt. Through an ultrasheer stocking, he felt her skin flinch, tightening in response. His chest constricted, and after waiting a heartbeat, he blew out a long, steady breath. When he glanced her way, it didn't help that his gaze landed on another of her sexy silk blouses, this one pale pink. With just a glance, he felt his hands itching to take it off.

Since the first night they'd spent together in her apartment, nearly a week ago, they'd been inseparable. Days were spent working, the nights making love in her apartment.

Only nine days remained until the Darden wedding, so all the major decisions had been made long ago. Now, everything was down to the nitty-gritty and fine tuning. Between meetings with other clients in the shop, Jimmy was accompanying Edie to Long Island, mostly to meet with subcontractors and to supervise the staff decorating the estate.

He'd even met Julia Darden, which was decidedly one of the stranger moments of his life. Given the numerous pictures he'd taken of her, he'd half expected her to recognize him, although she didn't, of course. Always, while canvasing Manhattan with his camera, he'd worn disguises, and while photographing the heiress, he'd posed as everything from a doorman, to a cabbie, to a homeless man. As she'd shaken his hand, her wide brown, doelike eyes had reflected no hint of recognition, but he'd realized he felt almost as if he knew her. He'd captured her essence on film for the public many times, and yet he'd been nothing more than a thorn in her side....

Odd, he thought now. Stranger still, that he hadn't pondered his motives for not sneaking a camera onto the premises, until now. After all, when he'd signed on at Big Apple Brides, that had been his initial intention. Now he was definitely more focused on what was happening between him and Edie. Within hours of making love, they'd each confessed overwhelming attraction. Each had been surprised by how much they had in common, although neither had mentioned it. "It's like we've been living parallel lives for years," Edie had whispered in awe once they'd risen from the living-room floor and snuggled together in bed.

"I didn't think I'd ever meet someone so much like me," he'd admitted.

She'd laughed. "I already have one twin. I never expected to find another."

"Weird, isn't it?" he'd murmured conversationally.

And it was. He'd never met anyone, for instance, who habitually leaped out of bed, threw on sweats and took a cab down Hudson Street in the middle of the night to buy Healthy Foods homemade ginger ice cream. It had turned out, that a place no one had ever even heard of—Lo Chin—was their favorite restaurant. They both rose at exactly six in the morning, without setting alarm clocks, and they shut their eyes at eleven at night, after which they usually slept like the dead.

And then there was the fact that he'd found two copies of the movie *Groundhog Day* next to her TV. Just as he did, she watched it whenever she was depressed, and they could both quote nearly every line. Not only that, but each had lost their first and second copies to malfunctioning video machines that had eaten the tapes. And what was the likelihood of that? Jimmy wondered now, making a mental note to buy Edie the movie on DVD since she'd just gotten herself a player.

Sighing, he glanced around the table, his heart swelling inside his chest because the scene made him miss his own folks in Ohio, especially since a traditional Thanksgiving dinner was being served. The holiday was long past, but this was apparently Joe and Viv's favorite menu, and according to Edie, it was served frequently. It reminded Jimmy of his parents, who'd be reclining right now in the La-Z-Boys Jimmy had just bought them and watching a big-screen TV he'd had delivered last Christmas. His jaw set as he pushed away thoughts of them, renewing his concentration on people at the table.

The other couples were seated on the opposite side, while Jimmy was sandwiched between Edie and her grandmother, a spry, elderly, birdlike Southern woman. Apparently something of a clotheshorse, she was dressed in a navy-and-white nautically inspired suit with matching two-tone pumps and a cap that was skewered to her blond ringlets by bobby pins. Earlier, after leaning a pearl-handled cane against a wall in the living room, she'd decided Jimmy would make a good substitute, and because she'd insisted on taking his arm, he'd wound up squiring her around during the visit and finally seating her, rather than Edie, for dinner.

By contrast to the formality of the elderly woman's

attire, Edie's father, Joe, who was seated at the head of the table, looked as if he'd just stepped from an old advertisement for Marlboro cigarettes. He was wearing jeans, a plaid flannel shirt and a baseball cap printed with a logo from Lorenzo Santini's hockey team. Given his no-nonsense wardrobe, not to mention his easy sense of humor, Jimmy couldn't help but think he'd hit it off famously with Jimmy's own pop, Edgar, just as Viv would with his mother, Jean.

Catching himself midthought, Jimmy realized he was already thinking in terms of a future with Edie, just as he was simultaneously admitting a long-term relationship was doomed to failure. Either he walked away soon, leaving her with pleasant memories about their time together, or he came clean about who he was, watched the proverbial mess hit the fan and let *her* end the relationship.

Whichever tack he took, the fact remained that he was conflicted because he really did want to shoot the Darden wedding. Fudging a résumé and calling in favors from ex-bosses who'd functioned as references hadn't been easy, but it had landed him the gig at Big Apple Brides. Even if he confessed what he'd done to Edie, he'd only walk away a double loser, since he was sure she'd never forgive him. Simply put, she was too good for him…too good to forgive a guy who'd stooped so low. *Damn my own calculating mind*, he suddenly thought. Sometimes, he really didn't like the guy he'd become….

"Who cooked?" Edie was asking between bites, glancing between her parents. "You or Dad?"

"Dad did the turkey," said Viv. "I did the rest."

Joe gaped at his wife in mock horror. "You will not take the credit for that strawberry cheesecake. If you try, I may take dessert into the den and eat it by myself." He laughed. "And *then* I'll divorce you."

"Promises, promises," quipped Viv.

"Please," argued Edie. "Make up, you two. At least long enough for me to get at the cheesecake. I'll never make it through another day of the Darden wedding without some comfort food in my stomach."

Before her father could answer, Marley groaned. "Dad, you know I can't eat dairy."

"Sorry, hon," returned Viv, "but your father and I agreed that we can only go so far to accommodate a vegan daughter. We draw the line at striking turkey and cheesecake from the Friday night menu."

"C'mon," complained Marley. "Just one tofu pie to prove your love."

"Next she'll want us to eat seitan burgers," said Bridget, forming a small O with her glossed lips and gesturing a perfectly manicured index finger toward it. "Gag," she continued as if she hadn't already made her point. "Give Marley an inch, Dad, and she'll take a mile."

"Bridget's right. The Bennings are all about conditional love, Marley, you know that," quipped Joe. "I will continue to love you only if I can eat my cheesecakes."

"Well, don't call me asking for free workouts when you get your cholesterol checked," said Marley.

"I liked you better when you fell off the wagon and were eating in fast-food joints," Joe continued in a mock grumble.

Marley just laughed. The transformation in her since Jimmy had first seen her some weeks ago on *Rate the Dates* was remarkable. During the show, she'd dressed like Edie, of course, since she'd pretended to be her sister, wearing conservative suits, blow-drying her shoulder-length hair, and doing her nails and makeup. Seen together, even dressed exactly alike, Jimmy had been able to tell the women apart, but now, they scarcely even looked like sisters.

Marley had quit straightening her hair, and now she was letting it dry naturally, so that wild curls cascaded around her face. Her face no longer showed traces of makeup, and while Edie wore a tailored skirt, Marley was clad in a warm-up suit with low-slung, bell-bottom pants.

The sisters did have one thing in common, however. Both looked radiant. *In love,* Jimmy mentally corrected. He glanced between them. Marley was taking healthy bites of the vegan-friendly portions of her meal with one hand, while linking the free arm through that of her dark-haired, dark-eyed fiancé, Cash Champagne. Edie was staring at Jimmy, smiling.

And Bridget looked just as happy. If it weren't for the shape of her face and her blond, blue-eyed coloring, the youngest Benning might look as if she'd come from another family, altogether. Stylistically, she was definitely something to behold, wearing a faux fur leopard-print top and floor-length black pleather skirt with pointy-toed boots that peeked out from beneath. She seemed more interested in kissing her fiancé, Dermott, than eating, and when she did bother to concentrate on food, most of it was delivered to a tawny pug dog named Mug, who'd been spinning in expectant circles at her feet, and who now scampered across the room, curled up near the fireplace and made a show of going to sleep.

Catching Edie's gaze, Jimmy realized she'd gotten distracted again, so he squeezed her knee under the table. "Quit worrying," he coaxed. "Worrying's not going to make the Darden wedding turn out any better."

"Good point," she murmured. "But I just remembered that I need to call a car service for the musicians. The other service canceled yesterday."

"Relax."

"I'm trying."

The Bennings' apartment was definitely the place to do it, he thought. It brimmed with positive energy, and he could almost feel the love the girls had grown up with. Although the temperature outside had risen to nearly sixty, as expected, the room was still scented by faint sweet wood smoke from the fireplace. As he began rubbing slow calming circles on her knee, his eyes trailed over a mantel decorated with family snapshots, then shifted to bookshelves crammed with well-read paperbacks and walls adorned with art that Edie and her sisters had made when they were kids.

Then his eyes settled on her again, just as she heaved a sudden sigh. Following her gaze, he winced, since it had strayed to a chair stacked with newspapers. Most were recent tabloids from the past few days, and all contained fairly explicit photographs of either Julia or Lorenzo. As if reading Edie's mind, Joe Benning said, "Keep the focus on doing the best job you can for the Dardens, Edie. You don't have any control over how other people interfere with the wedding."

Jimmy wanted to point out that Jack Stevens's motive was probably cold hard cash, not ruining the Darden wedding, but he bit his tongue, his eyes taking in the photograph on the top of the stack. It was of Julia staring into the mirror in what was identified as an executive bathroom inside the building of a major television network, where she'd gone to be with Lorenzo while he made a TV appearance. She was checking her teeth in a decidedly unflattering way, and that angered Jimmy. He'd shot celebrities, yes. But he'd never diminished them.

He wished he'd been able to find out more about Jack Stevens, too, but so far, the inquiries he'd made had rendered zilch. Overnight, the guy had come from nowhere and taken the celebrity photography scene by storm. Every day new, hard-to-get photographs were being sold to the tabloids, and rumor had it that monthly magazines had bought pictures, also. Most were of Lorenzo.

"I hope they don't give up and elope," Edie said, voicing her worst fears.

"After you've helped them plan the world's most gorgeous wedding for six months?" countered Viv Benning, who was still wearing a white chef's apron. "Don't even think it, Edie. Everything's going to be perfect."

"She's right. Come this Sunday, we're taking the rest of the stuff for the wedding to the estate," Joe coached. "We'll meet in front of your shop at ten, Edie. We might as well finalize the plans now. I meant to tell you earlier—I lined up guys to do the heavy hauling, the way you asked me to, and about the cake—"

"That can't go until the morning of the wedding," put in Viv. "I know Edie said they've got a freezer that's suitable, but…"

"Edie's having me make two cakes," Joe clarified. "Just in case. So, I thought we'd keep one at the Dardens' and one in the bakery."

"Well, that makes sense," agreed Viv.

"From what Pete Shriver says," continued Edie, as if

she hadn't heard a word her parents were saying, "nobody knows who Jack Stevens is. No one buying pictures for the tabloids had ever heard of him before. And nobody can figure out how he's getting close enough to get the pictures of Julia and Lorenzo."

"Other people, too," Jimmy pointed out.

"Mostly sports stars," continued Joe, returning to the earlier conversation. "I've been following the papers, too."

A barely discernible wounded quality crept into Edie's tone. "Why won't people just leave this alone! Julia's so nice. More than most, she deserves to enjoy her day in the sun. But she's getting increasingly upset, and I don't blame her."

"Even the nicest people can be provoked," agreed Viv.

"She's still getting letters...." Edie's voice trailed off.

Joe's voice sharpened. "Threatening her life?"

Edie nodded. "Pete keeps saying he thinks the threats are a hoax, that the letters are just a spiteful ruse calculated to unnerve everybody and ruin the wedding." She paused, shaking her head. "Photographers like Jack Stevens and Jimmy Delaney are just fanning the fire. What if things escalate, and someone actually does make an attempt on Julia's life?"

"Or what if they already did?" put in Marley. "I mean, I know Pete's view regarding the incident in the woods, but the fact remains that Julia and I were out there jogging when some guy fired off a few rounds several weeks ago."

"Why would anyone ruin such a beautiful day?" Edie repeated, her voice dipping so low that Jimmy barely heard it; it was almost as if she simply couldn't take in human spitefulness. Probably she couldn't, he decided. Nice people often couldn't imagine the baser motives of their fellows. And Edie, just like Julia, was definitely a nice person. "Oh—" she suddenly blurted distractedly, as if interrupting some internal monologue she'd been having with herself. "I completely forgot to mention this! Guess what!"

Everyone stared expectantly. "Remember the videographer who followed around Cash and Marley when they were on *Rate the Dates?*" Edie continued.

Cash and Marley groaned audibly, then Marley, said, "Vinny Marcel. Heavyset. Bearded. Endlessly annoying. How could we forget?"

Cash chuckled, absently toying with a plain tan tie he wore beneath a matching sport coat. "We must have run from him…what?" He glanced at Marley. "A hundred times?"

"Outfoxed him," Marley corrected. "While he was trying to take our picture."

"His name wasn't really Vinny Marcel," Edie announced. "Pete Shriver's been in contact with some media people. And he found out Vinny Marcel was really Jimmy Delaney, in disguise. I guess Jimmy Delaney thought Marley was me, and he started working on *Rate the Dates* as a videographer, hoping that by getting closer to me…"

"He'd get to Julia," Marley finished.

"The guy must be a really pathetic head case," muttered Edie. "Eleven orders of protection haven't kept him away from Julia Darden."

Jimmy winced, wishing a hole in the floor would open and swallow him.

"That totally sucks," Bridget commented. "You'd think the media would have respect for other people."

"He's probably rich as sin," added Marley.

"Well, maybe that's all such people have going for them," put in Viv. "Living vicariously through the celebrities they photograph."

Jimmy shifted uncomfortably in his chair, thankful when the conversation shifted to other aspects of the Darden wedding, including the music Dermott was arranging.

"Did you find something to wear to the rehearsal dinner next Saturday night?" asked Viv.

Edie nodded. She'd been looking for something fancy enough that she'd blend into a crowd of well-dressed guests, but that would also be comfortable, so she could work after the dinner without changing clothes. "I ordered a jersey knit dress online," she said, "and it got here yesterday. It's fine." She blew out another peeved sigh. "I just wish we didn't have to use the Darden's ballroom for both the rehearsal dinner and the wedding. We're going to be there all night, taking down the tables for the one event and setting up chairs for the next."

"We'll do a dry run with the guys I hired this weekend," assured Joe. "They'll have the dinner tables down and chairs set up for the wedding in just a couple of hours. It'll be a late night, but I think we'll be out by three in the morning."

Edie grunted softly, pressed fingers to her temples, then said, "I'm about ready for that cheesecake now, Dad."

As he rose to get it, Granny Ginny finished the last bite on her plate and set down her fork. Looking as if she'd had it with all the talk of a non-Benning wedding, she said, "When's the date for you two lovebirds, Seth?"

Jimmy had gotten so involved in the conversation that it took him a full moment to realize he was being addressed. "Why, I declare," Granny Ginny drawled, "I do believe the cat's got this poor man's tongue."

"Granny!" exclaimed Edie in censure, looking as if she was equally relieved to shift her attention from the Darden wedding. "Seth and I just met. He's working as my assistant until he finds other work and until I can get through the current crunch...."

But everybody at the table knew there was more to the story, Jimmy thought. He and Edie had spent every waking moment they weren't in the shop in bed together, and the energy sparking between them was unmistakable. He'd always considered himself a normal, healthy guy, but he'd had no idea he was capable of the kind of sexual stamina he'd experienced around Edie over the past few days. He'd been with countless women for a few months at a time. Basically, in bed, they each pulled out the sexual tricks they'd learned with partners, but then, they seemed to reach a point where all the old stuff was used up, and then the interest waned.

Already, he knew that would never be the case with Edie. With her, everything was completely different, just the way Ches had said things had been different with Elsa. In bed, he and Edie weren't trying to impress each other, only to have a good time. Pulling himself from the thoughts, he teased Granny, saying, "We're going to let you pick the date for us."

Granny Ginny's bright pink lips stretched into a grin over gleaming dentures. "Well, let's see..." She played along. "Unfortunately, April first is already taken by Julia Darden...."

"And Edie has to plan a wedding for me and Dermott before she starts on hers," protested Bridget.

"Ours, too," put in Marley. "And that should be the most important priority because—"

"But I'm the oldest," Edie interjected before Marley could finish. Whatever reticence she'd felt initially about joining the joking seemed to have passed. Even if she and Jimmy had only known each other a week, this was, after all, in jest. "So, Seth and I have to get married first. It's only fair."

"True," said Marley, "but…"

The hesitation and sudden seriousness in her voice got everyone's attention, and sounds of crinkling napkins, kisses and flirtatious under-the-table knee grabbing quieted. Edie squinted at her twin. "But?"

Tossing blond curls over her shoulder as she turned, Marley looked at Cash, who nodded. "Well," she said, "Cash and I have an announcement to make."

"Oh, honey," gasped Viv, as if sensing what was coming. There was a note of worry mixed with excitement in her voice, since Cash and Marley hadn't known each other long.

"Why," declared Granny Ginny with a throaty chuckle, "I knew Miss Marissa's wedding curse ended when Bridget got back from her ghost-busting trip to my plantation house in Florida!"

As if to prove it, Marley said breathlessly, "Cash and I are pregnant." Her words now came in a rush. "We were going to wait until after the Darden wedding to tell you. So much is going on around here right now. But…"

"We couldn't wait," Cash finished, his Louisiana drawl drawing out each word as he looped an arm around his fiancée's shoulders.

Leaning against his chest, she curled her head on his shoulder and smiled up at him. "Oh, Edie," she gushed as Joe and Viv rose and circled the table to hug the mother-to-be and her fiancé. "When the Darden wedding's over, will you think about helping Cash and me plan? We want a small wedding, and we want it before I'm really showing, so it'll have to be in the next couple of months."

"Maybe in June," said Cash, grinning as Joe clamped a hand down on his shoulder and squeezed, showing his affection. "That's traditional, right?"

"Cash has tons of friends in New Orleans, maybe even more than I have here," Marley plunged on, "so we might consider having the ceremony in Louisiana. Anyway, you and I will just have to talk it over...."

As Edie's twin rambled on, chattering about everything from the dress she envisioned for herself, to the kind of service she wanted, Jimmy's eyes drifted once more around the room. Yeah, the Bennings place was different from his folks'. Their lifestyles were different. But there were even more similarities, especially in the sense of community and love, and in the level of interest people took in each other. His parents mantel, too, was filled with cherished family photographs.

All of it seemed a far cry from the life he'd been living.

Suddenly glancing at Edie, Jimmy wished he really was the dream date he was calling Seth Bishop. As he took in her soft expression and the dancing warmth in her blue eyes, he thought of how she'd curled against his bare chest last night as she fell asleep, and he wanted his old life back. Right now, he could barely even remember the young man he'd been just seven or eight years ago, so idealistic and full of promise. Every moment he spent with Edie, he was starting to crave his old life even more....

6

HEARING SOMETHING behind her, Edie turned abruptly in the Darden's pantry, then she squealed. "You!" she exclaimed, laughing when Seth hugged her. "You scared the daylights out of me! I didn't even hear you come in!"

"It was intentional. I wanted to surprise you," he murmured, using the hard strength of his body to pin her against the counter. Pulling her into an embrace, he sprinkled kisses into her hair. Tilting back her head, Edie offered access to the slender column of her neck and was pleasantly rewarded when he looped wet kisses from her earlobe all the way down to where the top button of her blouse was undone. Releasing a throaty satisfied male sound, Seth glided his palms farther around her waist, and when he lowered them, cupping her behind, she felt her skirt rising dangerously high on her thighs. When he drew her even closer, their hips locked and her whole body flooded with gushing warmth.

Sucking in a quick breath, she arched, glancing toward the half-open door. His gaze meshed with hers, and she could tell he was wondering the exact same thing—if they could get away with making love. Simultaneously, they both burst out laughing.

"What a mind you have," he teased huskily.

"We've been working awfully hard," she murmured. "Maybe it's time for a reward." Casting another glance toward the door, she slipped a hand between them, found the fly of his jeans and squeezed.

Clearly affected, he said, "Too bad I hear people coming."

Realizing he was right, she touched him once more, leaving him with a promise and said, "Later then?"

His eyes lasered into hers. "Count on it."

"One night away from me was too much for you, huh?"

"Sure was." He paused. "Feel like a sleepover tonight?"

"I was taking that for granted."

But she'd wondered why he'd been unavailable Friday night. She'd hoped he'd agree to come in Saturday morning, too, to work some overtime. She'd needed to swing by her father's work space, and go over the menu for the rehearsal dinner a final time. Both had made a last-minute decision to provide an alternative dessert, and Julia had agreed, but after having dinner with her parents on Friday, Seth had merely kissed her at the door, saying he needed to go home.

"I've got plans tomorrow morning," he'd explained.

"Plans?" she'd asked, expecting him to become more specific.

He'd merely smiled as if he intended to keep his secret, and she'd found herself smiling back, deciding he was teasing her. "Trying to retain a sense of your mystery?" she guessed.

"Exactly."

"My guy, Garbo," she'd said, laughing, before he hovered closer and covered her mouth with his, kissing her deeply.

"Otherwise," he continued, his voice turning raspy

with need, "what would be left for you to discover about me in the second week of our relationship, Edie?"

She'd let him go without argument, knowing she'd miss having him in her bed, watching him walk into a night that had warmed considerably. The air was still sharp with hints of winter, but scents of spring had reached her nostrils, too, and she was glad to see that the recent frost and snow hadn't ruined the dogwoods planted in boxes along the sidewalk.

She'd told herself to go inside, but she hadn't. Oh, she'd known she was standing in the doorway, watching him like a lovesick fool, but she felt riveted to the spot as Seth Bishop crossed Hudson Street, clearly intending to catch a cab that could turn right and head east, since he lived in the East Village. As he stepped onto the curb and pivoted to face traffic, his eyes had found hers from across the four-lane street, and she'd heard Granny Ginny's words ring in her ears. *When's the date for you two lovebirds?*

He'd raised a hand to hail a cab, but then he'd turned it toward her, waving and grinning before returning his attention to the oncoming cars. For long moments after he'd gotten inside a cab, Edie had kept her eyes on the silhouette in the backseat until the car rounded a corner.

Just as it vanished from sight, Edie had whispered, "that's the man I'm going to marry."

She'd felt it deep in her bones. A romantic at heart, she'd read countless novels about love, and she'd even memorized some of the world's greatest poetry. She'd always believed in love at first sight, and as she'd stood in the doorway of the shop that had been her other life dream, Edie felt grateful that the experience of true love had finally found her. Her heart had swelled with joy. Maybe, just maybe, all her dreams were going to come true.

Now her eyes sharpened on Seth's. Glancing away from him, she looked toward the doorway that led to the professional kitchen. Beyond that, was a short service hallway that opened onto a large, empty space designed for entertainment, which the Dardens called the ballroom. She could hear voices coming closer, raised in anger.

She groaned. "What now?"

Seth stepped away. "I knew I heard someone coming."

"Julia and Lorenzo," she said, recognizing the voices. Lifting on her tiptoes, she kissed Seth quickly before abruptly heading for the door and leaving him to follow. "And Pete Shriver," Edie added, speeding her steps as she crossed the kitchen and entered the hallway. When she reached the ballroom, she realized she'd been holding her breath and exhaled slowly.

The place was in pandemonium. It was a beautiful room, surrounded on three sides with sloping glass windows that were inset by glass doors. Seeing them, she shook her head. Window washers had been due to clean them today, but had rescheduled for this coming Friday. Actually, that was better, since the wedding was on Sunday afternoon, but now she was worried some mishap would prevent them from coming....

Boxes were strewn across a white tile floor, and some of Edie's father's catering staff were unpacking dishes. White aisle runners were unrolled against one wall, and the hardware needed to build three outdoor tents was laid out neatly in another area. Wincing, Edie hoped there was some way she could move the argument elsewhere, away from employees, but she only shot Seth a helpless glance as Julia Darden headed for one of the glass doors.

As usual, Edie's breath was taken away. Beauty like Julia Darden's definitely took some getting used to. She was tall and willowy, graceful even when angry.

"I can't take any more of this!" she exploded, her voice uncharacteristically high-pitched, her usually smiling pink glossed mouth bunched into a tight dot of fury. She was wearing a Gore-Tex coat loosely over jeans that encased impossibly long legs, and her brown hair was gathered into a ponytail. "I don't want a bunch of guys with walkie-talkies at my wedding. It's ridiculous. This whole thing has gotten out of hand. You know I love Daddy, Pete, but you're making Lozo and I live like caged animals."

Lozo was her pet name for Lorenzo. He'd come to a standstill a few feet away from her, looking cautious as if he was afraid to come too much closer. Sometimes dubbed by the media as a Latin Lothario, he was dark and swarthy, with thick black wavy hair and sensuous lips. Wearing a baseball cap and sweatshirt bearing the logo for the hockey team on which he played, Lorenzo thrust his hands deeply into jeans pockets, not bothering to mask the worried expression on his face.

Pete Shriver, who looked like a G-man, with a buzz cut, nondescript gray suit, white shirt, plain tie and shiny dress shoes, took a deep breath. "We got another letter, Julia. So you're going to have to do as I say."

"Another letter?" murmured Edie.

"I don't care," Julia said. "The letters have been coming since October. And that photographer, Jack Stevens, has found some way to get close to me and Lozo. Why don't you work on that, Pete?"

"I am," he said calmly.

"I think it's really Jimmy Delaney," she said. "He's

the only person who'd stoop so low as to take a picture of me while I'm nail-flossing my teeth."

"The wedding is Sunday, Julia," Pete continued calmly. "Just seven days from now. You need to hang in there. This time next week you're going to be walking down an aisle in this very room."

Usually self-possessed, Julia held both hands outward, the fingers splayed as if to indicate that absolutely no one should take another step closer. "I just," she began, speaking succinctly, "want to go into Manhattan by myself for one hour. I want to forget all the threatening letters, this guy Jack Stevens and Jimmy Delaney. Okay?"

Everyone around her had frozen. Edie had stopped in her tracks with Seth beside her, and the employees who'd been unpacking lavender-rimmed white dishes had ceased their movements. "I feel like he's trying to talk a woman down from a window ledge before she jumps," Edie whispered to Seth.

"I can't let you go off by yourself," said Pete. "You know that, Julia. More than anyone, you understand the security risks."

She groaned. "You and Daddy are so paranoid." She glanced at Edie. "I'm so sorry," she said. "I know you're creating the most beautiful day possible for me, but I...I just have to get out of here...."

Sighing, Edie nodded, then she followed Pete's gaze past the windows to the lawn beyond. The estate was large enough that there were a number of road accesses. Because of the shape of the house, she could see smoke coming from the chimney of a more recent addition, a white-bricked room on the other side of the kitchen, which Sparky Darden used as a study. It was a saving grace that the elderly man was there, not here, where he'd no doubt be putting in his own two cents, probably worsening the situation.

"And don't try to follow me, Pete," Julia threatened.

"Us getting married and the wedding are two separate issues," Lorenzo ventured. "So, do you mind if I come with you, Julia?"

Crossing her two long braceleted arms over her waist, Julia stared a long, blank moment at her fiancé as if she'd never even seen him before. "I am going into Manhattan," she announced, still speaking succinctly, as if each letter was a sentence in its own right. "Alone. I am a separate person, Lozo. We are not joined at the hip."

Lorenzo made the mistake of grinning. "Well, sometimes…" he began with a sexual innuendo that only increased Julia's pique.

Clasping her hands tightly against her chest, she glared at Pete, then Lorenzo and said, "Am I really marrying you next week?"

"Oh, c'mon, Julia," said Lorenzo. "Lighten up. Pete's just doing his job."

Panic had edged into her voice. "Whose side are you on?"

"Yours, baby," he assured.

Not looking convinced, she only rolled her eyes, turned abruptly, and forcefully pushed through one of the glass doors, saying, "If I don't get out of here, I am going to go stark raving mad."

Edie groaned. With all her heart, she wished Viv were here. Maybe she could fix matters. Raised by a widower, Julia hadn't had much mothering, and she was negotiating a New York wedding by her lonesome. "Great," Edie whispered on a sigh, wondering what to do. Right now, feeling Seth's palm settle at the small of her back did nothing to mitigate her feelings of dread.

And then Pete brought a walkie-talkie to his lips and said, "Okay, boys. Julia just left. Do your job. Follow her. And get her back here as soon as possible. The paparazzi's having a field day lately, and we got another of those sick letters."

Catching Edie's gaze, he held up a sheet of white paper. On it, spelled in letters cut from a magazine by an Exacto blade, it said, *Stop the wedding or the bride will die.* Unfortunately, it wasn't the first such letter Edie had seen. And to think that they'd been coming since October....

Slowly, Edie panned her gaze around the room. All day, strangers had been milling about. Julia had been in and out of her gown at least four times. Apparently, a mishap Edie couldn't begin to understand might derail the shipment of some fish eggs that her father and Julia had decided he should fly in from Alaska the day of the rehearsal dinner, since both of them felt whatever fish had laid them put caviar to shame.

"If I were Julia Darden," she found herself announcing to nothing but the thin air, "I know I'd elope."

As soon as the words were out, she heard a soft chuckle. Seth leaned closer, whispering into her ear, "Yeah, but would you do it with a Neanderthal like Lorenzo?"

Once more, Seth Bishop had said exactly the right thing at exactly the right moment. Brute male strength mixed with what Edie's sister Marley always called "the dumb-guy appeal," was definitely Lorenzo Santini's selling point. He was perfect for Julia, who seemed prettier than she was smart, and genuinely warmhearted.

Shaking her head, Edie burst out laughing. "You're more my type."

His eyes sparked with intelligence. "Good."

She paused. "Julia's going to come back before next Saturday night, right?"

Gorgeous dark eyes stared levelly into hers and two warm hands settled on her shoulders, squeezing tightly as Seth drew her nearer. "Yes," he repeated in a way that almost made her believe it. "Julia is going to come back before the rehearsal dinner."

"Thank you for the support," she whispered simply.

"Anytime," he whispered back.

"I CAN'T BELIEVE it's Wednesday," Edie said breathlessly, a few nights later, reaching a long bare arm and gripping her hand around one of the tall posters of her bed, glancing from Seth to the windows, sighing. They'd had dinner with her parents again tonight, and she really couldn't believe how Seth had hit it off with them. Sometimes, the Darden wedding actually seemed light-years away. Edie, herself, had met such a dream man....

Through the filmy gauze of sheer curtains, she could see hazy starbursts of streetlights that were barely discernible from the spray of bright white twinkling stars. Silver-tinged puffy clouds were unfurling in the dark like windblown sails billowing under the moon, and since she'd extinguished all the lights inside the room, then lit ten tea candles that flickered from various surfaces—tabletops and windowsills—those, too, were reflected in the windows, shining in the glass. "They're saying the weather's going to hit seventy on Sunday," she continued. "So maybe we can have the reception outside. I hope so. The sky looks clear now, but it said in the paper that it might rain."

Seth paused in the doorway. "It won't."

"You promise?"

"Yeah."

"You're a real godsend, do you know that? What would I have done over the past week and a half without you?"

He smiled. "Who knows?"

"I'm serious, Seth."

He merely shrugged. He was shirtless, his muscular chest bare. A rounded shoulder rested against the door frame and his belt had been removed, so his slacks rode down low on his hips. He looked delicious, lounging there, silhouetted in the semidarkness, a black line of wild curling hair bisecting his pecs and arrowing downward as if pointing the way to the most intimate part of him.

Just looking at him made everything inside her ache and grow tight, and she felt strangely surprised; she'd never felt this way about a man. Affected when one touched her, of course. But she'd never actually *ached* with anticipation. Her core was melting. The tips of her breasts were taut. A hand rested on her bare thigh, mostly to calm her nerves. And yet she wanted to draw this out, tease herself with his presence—to look her share, drinking in every inch of him with her eyes until the moment when she undressed.

His gaze was as warm as the candlelight that fluttered on his skin, and it was fixed where she was lying in bed, propped against pillows piled high against the headboard; her feet were resting on the edge of a white duvet turned back on pale pink sheets. Taking in the open bottle of champagne and two long-stemmed crystal glasses dangling from his fingers, she frowned in censure. "Correct me if I'm wrong, but I think that was for the Darden wedding."

A smile lifted his lips, but didn't meet his dark eyes, which were smoldering. "What did they order?" he asked rhetorically. "A hundred cases?" He shrugged. "I decided they wouldn't miss one itty-bitty bottle."

She couldn't help but smile. "You're positive about that?"

"Yeah. And this was a premeditated act," he admitted. "I even chilled the bubbly a couple of hours ago." He wagged his eyebrows. "Somehow, I figured we'd wind up in bed."

"You must be clairvoyant."

He nodded. Tucking the bottle under his arm, he reached for a radio on top of a dresser and flicked it on, tuning until he found classical piano music. "It came to me in a dream," he murmured lazily, as if in a trance. "You were going to strip for me before tying me to the bed and tongue kissing me from head to foot."

"Funny," she countered. "I thought that was what you were going to do to me."

He shook his head. "Nope. I saw the future first."

"You never should have gotten into the wedding business," she said, shutting her eyes and rubbing her temples. "Ah. I see it now," she announced, opening her eyes. "You're supposed to open a new age shop on West Fourth Street. You know, next to all the tarot card and palm-reading places."

"I'd watch you striptease all day in my crystal ball."

"You naughty boy."

"You don't know the half of it."

She crossed her arms, knowing full well the gesture

lifted her breasts, accentuating cleavage. "I've gotten hints." She added. "A striptease. Is that your heart's desire."

"And body's."

His eyes drifted slowly over her, creating a trail of burning fire, making her glad she'd slipped into sexy lingerie. She had a drawerful, and although the items had cost a fortune, she'd rarely worn any of them. She hadn't bought them to please any particular man, after all, but only because she was a romantic at heart. She loved the colors and textures of lace satin, not to mention the inventive touches with which high-fashion designers embellished delicate clothes. The sheer white short robe she wore half-open over a black bra and panties was definitely getting Seth's attention, just not enough that he'd left his post in the doorway, at least not yet.

She frowned. "What's bothering you?"

"Why do you ask?"

She sent him a long look. "Uh...because I'm lying here wearing next to nothing and you're still on the other side of the room. To me, that seems like a bit of a problem."

"Sorry," he murmured, chuckling softly as he used a shoulder to push away from the doorjamb. Stopping beside the bed a moment, he set down the bottle and glasses, then poured their drinks. She took one from him, registering the warm feel of his dry palm as it traced the back of her hand, then the cool, effervescent liquid as she sipped. Feeling his eyes on her skin again, she realized they were warming every place they touched—the curving line of her neck, the swell of her breasts.

"Really," she said. "What's on your mind?"

He considered a moment as he got into bed and rolled on his side next to her, propping himself on an elbow, his eyes just inches away. "Jack Stevens," he finally said as he traced a finger over her collarbone.

Turning her body toward his and lifting her hips, she smiled. "I thought we weren't supposed to talk about work."

"Something you'd rather do?" he asked lazily.

Slipping a hand between them, she silently urged him to give her some more room, feeling the taut muscles of his abdomen flinch against her knuckles as she flicked open the button of his pants. Blowing out a long breath, she glanced downward as she found the zipper and tugged. For once, she really didn't want to talk about someone else's wedding or romance. She just wanted...

"Here," she coaxed as the zipper hit bottom, a tuft of his white briefs becoming visible as his erection burgeoned through the open V. Shutting her eyes to bliss, Edie took a deep breath, pulling the scent of arousal deeply into her lungs as she molded her fingers over white cotton, touching him, feeling him tighten in her hand, growing harder, hotter. Opening her eyes, she surveyed her handiwork. "Still want to talk about Jack Stevens?" she asked raspily.

That got a smile out of him. Even though he shook his head, he said, "It's just that..." Suddenly shuddering, he lifted his hips for her touch, then sucked a sizzling breath through clenched teeth. "That you said Pete Shriver's never heard of him before."

"Him who?"

"Jack Stevens."

She was edging the trousers over his hips, and her heart was hammering hard, taking her breath. Truly, he was something to behold, his skin dusky, the darkening erection springing from all those wild curls. As he kicked off the pants and they tumbled over the edge of the mattress, she said, "You don't really want to talk about Jack Stevens."

She definitely didn't. And yet she was beginning to think maybe there was something she could do to make him stop taking the pictures. Maybe she'd ask Pete more about where Jimmy Delaney was teaching, track him down and see if he had any ideas about how to find Jack....

But those were thoughts for another day. Seth's eyes had darkened, sharpening with awareness. Lowering his head, he brought his lips so close to hers that she could feel the heat of his breath fanning on her mouth in the second before he kissed her. She moaned when their lips touched. His mouth was so heavenly, his tongue scalding. She felt as if she were blistering, inside and out.

His hand glided under her chin, his fingers slowly stroking the line of her jaw, and his tongue plunged deeper, more savagely, turning demanding as fire exploded in her belly. Dripping thick and molten, it curled through her limbs, and when he molded a hand over her panties, her mound swelled, full to bursting. Perspiration beaded everywhere at once—on her lip, the nape of her neck, the back of her knees.

Suddenly, she broke the kiss, whispering, "I wouldn't want to disappoint your crystal ball."

With that, she stood and slipped into some black come-love-me stilettos she'd left tucked under the bed, then moved her hips, catching the slow, sensual rhythm of the music, swaying as she stepped backward, taking long-legged dance steps away from the bed, so he could better watch her....

And she him. He'd rolled to his back, his aroused body dark in the candlelight, darker still against the pale covers. She could tell he was breathless; his chest was rising and falling rapidly, and his hand gave one barely perceptible shake as he slid it into his chest hair, fisting his fingers before absently stroking a pectoral, strumming his own skin as his unblinking eyes fixed on her body. After lightly licking his lips, he spoke, his voice as low as the music. It seemed to roll toward her on a wave of piano notes. "Dance for me," he murmured hoarsely.

Undulating her hips, she widened her stance, the long muscles of her thighs working, brushing each other then parting, as she swayed from side to side. Splaying her hands on her thighs, she let them travel upward, making the transparent robe rise a tantalizing inch.

"Higher," he said almost roughly.

He looked mesmerized as she complied, toying with the sash of the robe now, then untying it. Moving with slow, sweet deliberation, she took the ends of white silk in each hand, then stepped through the loop she'd created. With one hand in front of her and one behind, she slid the white ribbon back and forth, sawing it under the black panties she wore, teasing herself until she thought she might explode, then she pulled the sash taut, wedging it, making her cleft visible for him, feeling herself gush into the black silk.

"Oh, Edie," he said simply, his jaw slackening, his eyes half shutting in ecstasy, the hand on his thigh tightening now, his long fingers digging into his flesh. "Do it, baby. C'mon. Show me how you dance. Dance for me."

Heat burst inside her. She'd never entertained a lover like this, and she was loving every minute of it. No man had ever looked so utterly interested. Or aroused. Circling her hips, grinding the air in slow, undulating circles as if making love to him, she edged the robe off her shoulders, then replaced the see-through fabric immediately, only to let it drop once more.

"Lower," he urged. "Lower…"

"Just tell me what you want," she whispered.

"Lower," he whispered back.

Until she'd slid the robe all the way down her body and dropped it to the floor. "Turn for me," he muttered, his voice catching, turning ragged. "Let me see the back."

She did, and when she was facing him again, she splayed her hands on her ribs, then pushing them upward, stopped the second before she caught the sloping undersides of her breasts, prompting him to say, "Oh, yes."

"You like my dance?"

"Don't stop," he said, his voice hushed with need that pushed her further toward the brink. She was loving the rush of doing this, and she wanted more. Once more, she realized she wanted to explore everything with this man…to let him take her to whatever dangerous heights they could scale together. "Touch yourself," he encouraged. "Let me see you get hot, Edie…really hot."

He didn't want her holding back, so she didn't. She was burning as she squeezed her breasts, pressing them together before bending way down for him, showed him her cleavage. Knifing her fingers, she slid them into the cleft, slowly thrusting, letting him imagine himself thrusting between her breasts until he uttered a harsh ecstatic sound.

When she heard it, she reached behind, unhooked the back of the bra, then slid the straps down her arms. Moving her shoulders in a steady shimmy, she shook rhythmically, the aching taut nipples freed now—so dark, dusky and hurting for his mouth.

"C'mere," he suddenly said. "Come to bed."

But she only plucked the nipples for him instead, wetting her fingers, then rolling the tips between them until they were unbearably stiff. She, too, was starting to whimper, unable to hold back, her body impossibly aroused.

"Come to bed," he urged hoarsely. "I need you now, Edie. I need you...."

Caressing herself, she folded both hands over her breasts, squeezing hard until he cried out once more, his hand suddenly moving over his erection. Shuddering, he inhaled sharply as long strong fingers gripped where he'd gotten so hard, not stroking, but squeezing tight as if he could no longer stand the torture of this dance she wasn't about to stop, not now, she thought...not now, when his head was tilting back in pleasure, his eyelids dropping, the tip of his wet tongue circling his lips, going around and around....

She'd never imagined anything this hot. She turned for him, seesawing the sides of the black panties, so the silk slid over one cheek, then another, her skin coated with a sheen of perspiration now, whether from the exertion of dancing or from what she was doing to herself—to both of them—Edie wasn't sure. Shifting from one stiletto to the other, she turned to face him, feeling raw as she pushed the panties all the way down her silken thighs to her knees....

She stepped out of them. She danced toward the bed again, the scent of their bodies exploding, filling her. Balancing on one leg, she lifted the other high, crooking her knee, so she could hook the heel of her shoe over the footboard of the bed, giving his eyes full access.

HE WAS BESIDE HIMSELF. His shaking fingers curled hard on his erection and he released another guttural sound. When she slowly, purposefully pushed a manicured finger inside, it was finally too much. Getting out of bed, he circled the mattress and came behind her, urging her back. Her long legs were still dangling over the side, her heels brushing the floor, when he entered her with a long unbroken stroke that pushed them to the brink. He kept her right there, flying on the edge, the seamless joy carrying them both to oblivion as he buried himself, his body locked to hers, inseparable, as deep as it could go. And then, somehow, he went deeper still. They were one, she thought. One.

And then she broke. Senseless words erupted. Suddenly, she was begging him, her shattered mind coming completely apart, like broken glass. Like a ribbon, she was undone. She had to feel him do that to her again. It was an obsession. A need that simply couldn't be denied. "Just once more," she begged. "Once…once more…"

His thighs shaking, straining, he pulled back, a trembling hand splaying on her taut belly, then lowering, inching downward until the thumb dipped into where their bodies were joined and he found the turgid nub of her pleasure. She gasped as his thumb pressured her, her hands sinking into the sheets and gathering them in fistfuls as he rubbed deep circles. Only then did he thrust again with a slow, sure rhythm, the way she'd just asked…going deeper, harder. He stretched and filled her.

But she barely knew it. This felt like her very first time. And her last. She'd never want another man. Everything, from now on, would involve him.

The world she'd known before Seth Bishop was gone.

7

PAULIE SAMONELLI was the least likely florist Jimmy had ever laid eyes on. Short and heavyset, he looked like an Italian Buddha, but with a mop of black hair and a full dark beard. Most of his hair was tucked beneath a navy sailor's cap, which he wore pulled down low, so the bill nearly obscured beady dots of black eyes. If someone had told Jimmy that Paulie was a Mafia hit man, bar bouncer, or henchman for union workers, Jimmy would have believed them.

"Okay, Paulie," said Edie, suddenly shivering. "Everything's all set then?"

Jimmy slid an arm around Edie's waist and drew her against his side as they continued walking through Paulie's refrigerated warehouse toward the front door. The place was on Ninth Avenue, near the Hudson River, banked by windows and crammed with every variety of flower under the sun. "Cold, huh?" he murmured.

"Freezing," she said.

Briskly, Jimmy rubbed his arm up and down the sleeve of a navy crepe dress printed with tiny white flowers. They'd walked the few blocks from Big Apple Brides, and because the temperature was in the sixties, she'd left her coat at the shop, not anticipating how cold it would be in the warehouse. Easily, it was forty degrees.

"Like I said, Edie, I won't have your order until the day of." Paulie thrust both beefy hands deep into the pockets of threadbare jeans, surveying rows of flowers with a proprietorial air as they passed. Too heavy to button his jeans jacket, he wore it open over a red, waffled long-john shirt that, in turn, had gaping buttons. "I think we did all right for you when *Celebrity Weddings* interviewed me and took those shots of the warehouse. It was lucky for me, too, Edie. I got some business when they ran the story."

"Great," said Edie.

"I owe you one," he returned. "We'll cut your stems, have 'em all ready to go by nine, and my truck will be out on Long Island by noon. The closer to showtime, the better they'll look."

"And Saturday night?" She groaned, then muttered rhetorically. "Pinch me. Is this really going to happen tomorrow night?"

"The rehearsal dinner's at five, right?"

She nodded. "Unless something goes wrong."

"Nothing will go wrong," Jimmy put in.

Paulie nodded sympathy. "I keep seeing those trashy pictures in the tabloids, Edie. It can't be easy. But everything will work out. I've done bigger events than the Dardens'. You can count on the flowers."

She sighed. "I know. I just wish there was some way to track down Jack Stevens. He's the guy taking most of the pictures. Darden security is even willing to buy him off, I think."

Paulie squinted. "You mean, pay him not to take pictures?"

"Maybe. Julia feels...like she's under siege."

"She is," the florist sympathized. "But it's only another couple days. Then they're on their honeymoon. Where did you say they were going?"

"St. Martin for now. Lorenzo's doing some advertisements associated with the hockey team—something to do with sneakers and sports clothes. When he's done, they're going to Europe."

"At least you guys got rid of that Delaney character."

Edie nodded. "Apparently, he got a tough judge. Diana Little. She once wrote a book called *The Wrongdoers*."

"He got hard time, huh?"

She shook her head. "Community service. But at least for the moment, he seems to have taken it to heart. A guy on the Darden security staff filled me in the other day. He's teaching photography to juvenile delinquents for the next few weeks, at least on weekends."

Paulie shook his head in disgust. "Ask me, they ought to string guys like that up by their thumbs, not expose kids to them. But that's just my humble opinion. I'm no lawman."

"And I'm glad you're a florist," assured Edie with a smile. "About the rehearsal dinner," she continued, returning to the previous topic. "It's a three-hour event after the rehearsal, itself—dinner and speeches. Then Julia's having people in for dancing and a buffet dessert. It's a sort of preparty." When Paulie frowned, Edie shrugged. "Julia said she couldn't stand going to all the trouble of decorating, serving food and dressing to the nines only for the wedding party. So, as we discussed, we need the lilies on Saturday, and all those white roses on Sunday."

"Who's coming to the party after the rehearsal?"

"Extended friends. Some media people. Lorenzo's manager, coaches and teammates. They've been told to come and leave on time, and I'm sure they will. That party's scheduled from eight to eleven."

Paulie exhaled in a low wolf whistle. "Then your dad's people are breaking down the room, cleaning it and setting up again?"

"It's got to be ready by the next morning. The wedding's not until three, but we have deliveries coming starting around six the next morning when the tents go up. We don't want to put down the aisle runners until last. Same with the indoor garden arbor—they're taking their vows under it."

Despite his pique over the comments about him, and his strong wish to break his silence and defend himself, Jimmy almost smiled, careful not to forget he was supposed to be Seth Bishop. Edie was speaking by rote, clearly having given descriptions regarding the event countless times. She'd been living this wedding for months, even in her dreams.

"Guess you won't be sleeping Saturday, doll," said Paulie.

"Not until next week," agreed Edie as they crossed the threshold leading into the main office. Glancing between Jimmy and Paulie, she said, "I'll be right back. Little girls' room."

"I'll be waiting," Jimmy said.

After Edie excused herself, Paulie did the same, thrusting a beefy finger into the air next to Jimmy's face, as if to say he'd just thought of something important. "Be right back," he muttered gruffly. Abruptly turning, he barreled down a row stacked with open boxes full of long-stemmed, tropical flowers.

Sighing, Jimmy turned his attention back to Edie as she headed for a hallway on the other side of the office.

The place was made for warehousing flowers, which meant the flowers were, by far, the prettiest thing inside, besides Edie. Today was one of the few times he'd seen her in a dress rather than a suit and it flattered her. Clinging in the all the right places, it moved with the gentle sway of her hips, making the hem swish against the backs of her knees. Her straight, blond, blow-dried hair brushed her shoulders, moving in tandem, as if every part of her was dancing to unheard music. In a plain room with cinder block walls, she stood out like a burning torch.

He thought of the striptease she'd performed for him earlier in the week, felt his body grow tight, then suddenly startled, feeling a hand clamp down on his shoulder. "Here," said Paulie.

"Hmm?" Turning, Jimmy felt his lips part in surprise as the other man pressed a bouquet into his hand. He had no idea what the flowers were, but Paulie knew his business and they were beautiful. Large, waxy, white petals were shot through with dried navy flowers. "It'll match her dress," he said.

"Yeah. Pretend you thought of it," said Paulie. He flashed a grin, exposing two gold teeth.

Jimmy couldn't help but laugh. "I'd never have taken you for such a romantic, Paulie."

The other man shrugged, throwing up both hands, palms out. "What can I say?" he asked rhetorically. "Three ex-wives, seven kids, four girlfriends right now. Go figure."

Chuckling, Jimmy shook his head. "What's your secret?"

Taking him seriously, Paulie considered a moment, then said, "Honesty. I know plenty of guys with four

girlfriends, but they keep it under wraps. Me? I tell
them. Hey, I'm playing the field. The women," he continued, "they never feel bad if they know the truth."

"I'll keep that in mind."

"Honesty," Paulie repeated.

Not exactly Jimmy's strong suit.

"You owe me one," Paulie said. "Those are Edie's fa-
vorites." With that, he turned to go, jerking his head
away from the office, toward the warehouse. "I've gotta
unpack the rest of my boxes, so give my regards to the
looker when she comes out of the ladies'."

"Sure will."

Taking a deep breath, Jimmy stepped through the
front door of the warehouse and into the midday sun.
For a moment, he shut his eyes, tilted back his head and
let the warm rays play on his face. When he opened his
eyes again, he was staring toward the Hudson, and
when he glanced to his right, he was taking in the Chelsea Piers where he'd shot one of his more famous photographs of Julia Darden.

Guilt twisted inside him. Immediately shaking off
the feeling, he tried to concentrate on the shimmering
steely tidewaters that looked shot through with silver-
white streaks of light. Swells broke near the seawall, and
further out, he could see yachts and barges, even a few
sailboats. Gulls swooped overhead, then dived. Spring
seemed to have arrived overnight. And now, in just a
couple hours, he'd be eating dinner at Edie's folks just
as he had the previous Friday. After that, he was teaching the kids again—this would be his third Saturday—
and then Saturday night, he'd be expected at the Darden
rehearsal dinner.

He half turned as the door opened, then shut behind

him. Edie slipped her arm through his, shivering. "I should have brought my coat with me. It was freezing in there."

She sucked in a breath as he kissed her, pressing the flowers into her hands. He was sure he'd never seen anything so beautiful as when she ducked her head into the white petals, whispering, "They smell like heaven."

Wrapping an arm around her, he drew her more fully into an embrace, his heart swelling. The moment was so perfect. The sky was cloudless and blue over the water, the sun shining, and the most gorgeous woman in the world was beaming at him, looking like a bride, herself.

"Thank you," she whispered.

He shook his head. "No, thank *you*."

"For what?"

How could she even ask? "The past two weeks."

Brushing his lips across hers once more, he tried not to think of what was going to happen next. Deep down, he supposed he'd decided not to shoot the wedding. If the truth be told, he wished he wasn't going to the Darden estate again at all, not that it mattered. He'd always dressed in disguises, so the chances of anyone recognizing him were nil. Besides, he had to go. At this point, Edie was relying on him. Without a personal assistant to help with last-minute details, she'd have difficulty pulling everything together. But at some point, he really did have to tell her who he was…

He pulled back a fraction, his heart missing a beat. Should he say something now? Or would that only put additional pressure on her right before the wedding? Paulie had said he kept his girlfriends by being honest, but Jimmy hardly wanted to see Edie's blue eyes touched by pain, or her mouth slacken in wounded surprise. "Edie," he forced himself to say, anyway, testing the waters, "I've got something to tell you...."

Her voice hitched. "Me, too. Oh, Seth—" She slipped an arm around his waist, snuggling close so their bodies were flush and nearly crushing the fresh flowers between them. "I don't really know how to say it," she began again. "But you're so special. I mean, the past two weeks have been like a dream for me—"

"Same here," he assured.

"Really?"

Using a finger to brush a lock of hair from her temple, he nodded. "Years ago, when Ches met Elsa, he said it was like this for him. He said he felt as if he'd already known her for years. They just seemed to—"

"Fit?"

"Like a hand in a glove. They're on the same wavelength, somehow. My parents are like that."

"Mine, too. And I think we're like that," she murmured softly.

"And when we make love..." His voice trailed off, the memories of what they'd shared making him feel hot and cold, all at the same time, as if some internal thermometer monitor had just malfunctioned. "We need to talk," he began again.

His heart suddenly aching, Jimmy captured her mouth once more. After locking her lower lip between his lips, he lightly pushed his tongue where she'd parted for him, powerless but to lean more weight against her, the sharp pang at his groin demanding it, his pulse skyrocketing when she tilted her hips up to his.

"There's so much I want to tell you, too," she murmured against his dampened lips.

His mind felt lazy, zapped by the warm sun, the scent of flowers and her kiss. "Like?"

"I love you, Seth," she said simply.

Warring emotions came back to him, full force. A voice inside him screamed, *Tell her now. Maybe it's not too late.* Instead, his voice caught and he found himself saying, raspily, "I love you, too, Edie."

"HEY, DELANEY, where have you been lately, man?"

"Out and about," he forced himself to say later that night, not bothering to turn around, but glancing above rows of liquor bottles in front of him, into the Suds Bar's mirror as Benny, Alex and Tim approached. Ches was seated beside him, on a bar stool, and Jimmy couldn't help but notice how much more respectable his best buddy looked than the photographers.

Ches, who'd spent the day in court, was wearing a tailored, three-piece suit, with a lemon-yellow tie while Benny and Alex were clad in threadbare jeans and T-shirts. Tim was outfitted as a homeless man, swallowed by an overcoat far too heavy for the weather. All had cameras slung over their shoulders.

Jimmy half turned to look at them. "How's it hanging, guys?"

"Good," said Tim. "There was a red-carpet gig up on Seventy-Second Street. A fund-raiser. I got some hot shots of Nicole Kidman."

"But can they compare to shots of J. Lo stepping from the shower?" asked Alex.

Even as his pulse picked up, Jimmy damned himself for feeling an adrenaline rush. He glanced at Alex. "You didn't."

Alex nodded. "She was in a hotel. I paid off room service and took in her dinner."

"Which brings us to you, Delaney," said Tim, jerking his chin in the direction of the booths behind him as he unbuttoned the heavy coat. "We're going to grab a booth and share some pitchers. Unless you and Ches are having some deep discussion about your legal troubles, come on over and entertain us."

"Yeah," put in Alex. "We need an explanation from you. Over the past two weeks, you've disappeared from the scene, and, well…we're convinced you're doubling as this guy Jack Stevens."

Jimmy was stunned. "Me? Are you kidding? I'm the one who called you guys, asking if you'd ever heard of him."

The three men merely stared at him pointedly. Finally Benny said, "A ruse, we decided."

Jimmy's lips parted in astonishment. "You really think I'm selling pictures of Julia Darden under an assumed name?"

"Orders of protection never stopped you before," reminded Tim.

True. And maybe they hadn't this time. His relationship with Edie had, however. And yet the fact remained. He did make his living as a celebrity photographer, and sooner or later, he was going to have to eat. Glancing down, he toyed with the cocktail napkin under his imported beer, then turned his attention to the three men again. "I can see I really inspire trust," he couldn't help but say ruefully. Even his own partners in crime didn't trust him to tell the truth. *Pretty lousy, Delaney,* he thought. "I'm not taking pictures right now," he clarified.

"Yeah, yeah, yeah," pattered Benny, offering another

jerk of his chin before turning, casting a wave over his shoulder and heading toward a booth. "Come over in a while, you two. Shoot some darts."

"Maybe." Jimmy's tone was noncommittal. After a moment, he realized Ches was studying him and lifted an eyebrow in question.

"What's going on?" When Jimmy didn't respond, Ches looped a finger around the long neck of his beer and took a drink.

"What do you mean? What's going on?"

"The other morning, I stopped by to deliver some legal papers and just missed you coming out of your place. You were hailing a cab on Avenue B. So, I..." Ches paused. "Hailed another cab and followed you. When I saw you get out at Edie Benning's business..."

Jimmy uttered a low expletive.

"Are you doing what those guys suggested?" Ches persisted. "If you're taking pictures and selling them under another name right now, I need to know. Not as your buddy. As your lawyer."

Jimmy sent Ches a long look. "No."

Ches didn't look particularly convinced. He continued. "I gotta tell you, Jimmy, I love you like the brother I've never had, but I'm limited in how many times I can get you out of these jams. Regarding the current order of protection, we'll win on appeal. You're actually in the right, but..."

Ches shifted uncomfortably on the bar stool. "Hell, Jimmy," he suddenly said. "What are you doing with your life? When all this started, there were reasons for it. You had to make money fast, but now..." He glanced over his shoulders. "Those guys aren't bad guys, but they don't have the kind of talent you do."

Jimmy's throat felt tight. Next to his own father, Ches was the person he respected most in the world. Hesitating a moment, he said, "I took a job at Big Apple Brides, hoping to get close to Julia, I admit it. But now, I...I've been dating Edie Benning."

Ches gasped. "You're kidding."

"Nope."

And more than that, he thought silently. Quickly, he'd become a part of her life. Eating Friday night dinner with her family tonight had felt as ordinary as breathing, and now he wanted nothing more than to drown his sorrows because dread was filling him. Somehow, he had the sneaking suspicion that something was going to give soon—and once it did, he wouldn't be invited back to eat with Edie's family next week. Or any week after.

Ches sighed. "She doesn't know who you really are?"

Jimmy chewed the inside of his cheek. "Not a clue."

A long silence ensued.

"It gets worse," Ches finally said.

Jimmy couldn't imagine it. "How?"

"I'm going to have to leave you to drown your sorrows with the Neanderthals behind us. As much as I'd love to stick around, play darts and down some brewskies, I promised Elsa I'd watch the babies tonight, so she can go to a movie and get some alone time." He glanced at his watch, winced and suddenly stood. "I should have left fifteen minutes ago, bud."

"I've got school in the morning, anyway," Jimmy said.

At that, Ches laughed. "I bet that's something to behold."

Hearing the tone, Jimmy had to fight annoyance. It was as if Ches couldn't begin to imagine how Jimmy would fare in a roomful of kids, despite the fact that Ches's own sons adored being cuddled by him. Did he really think he was the only one of them who was going to find love and settle down? "Kids love me."

Ches eyed Jimmy a long moment. Before he turned to go, he said, "Then maybe you should consider becoming a schoolteacher for real."

"So, HAS EVERYBODY written down their secret vote for best picture?" Jimmy asked the next morning.

"Yes, Mr. Delaney," said some voices in unison, the loudest of which was the squeal of a little girl named Melissa Jones, who made him grin every time he looked at her. Dark skinned and scrawny with shoulder-length pigtails strung with beads, she clearly favored trendy clothes, and today she was wearing black pleather pants with a fringe-hemmed jacket. She was as sweet as sugar, so it was hard to imagine what she could have done wrong, although Jimmy had slowly realized the kids were hardly what his mind had conjured when he'd heard the term "juvenile delinquents." Most just seemed bored, in need of more positive outlets and probably had parents who weren't as accessible as they could be, for whatever reason.

"Okay. Fold up all the secret ballots and pass them up front."

As the kids did so, he stared down the long line of black-and-white photographs propped against the chalkboard. They were surprisingly good, and as he looked at them, he found himself wondering if he'd ever have kids of his own. Edie had said she wanted a family, and it was so easy to envision starting one with her. He'd like to play with his own, not Ches and Elsa's for a change....

He'd forgotten how inventive kids could be. Last week, as they'd developed pictures for the first time, he'd been astonished to see the images his wayward students had captured on film. Plenty of older, more technically accomplished people couldn't produce photographs as interesting. Truly, he thought now, children were the eyes of the world. Adults stayed too busy to look. But kids always saw far more than adults gave them credit for.

He took in a comical picture of a woman on the subway, surreptitiously trying to fix a garter. Another depicted a kid, probably about three years old, who was licking the head of a golden retriever that was tied to a parking meter. Clearly, the kid had decided to meet the dog on its own level.

Melissa's picture of her parents was the best, although he doubted the kids would vote for it. Rather than humor, it held deep poignancy. Intentional or not, she'd managed to get a good soft-focus shot, and since the couple was in an embrace, their faces weren't really visible. By taking it in affluent surroundings, Melissa had managed to bring the items surrounding the couple into much sharper focus. It was almost as if she was trying to say that material belongings had become more important than the relationships. In addition, she'd done an interesting job with a homeless man, showing his slow transformation as he got off the streets, and the series of pictures showed perception beyond her years.

Suddenly, he did a double take, belatedly realizing that some movement in the corner of his eye had captured his attention. Gazing through a window of the Little Red Schoolhouse, onto a park at the corner of Bleeker

Street and Sixth Avenue, he suddenly realized why he'd looked, then shook his head to clear it of confusion. For just an instant, he could have sworn he'd seen Edie in the park across the street. Something, he wasn't sure what, had convinced him she was there. Maybe a flash of wine-red, the color of a jacket she sometimes wore? A glimpse of blond hair?

His eyes scanned the landscape, but he didn't see her. Maybe it wasn't his imagination. Her shop was only about six blocks away. Still, six blocks in New York was different from six blocks in Ohio. So, what was Edie doing over here?

Memories of the previous day flitted into his mind, as stark as the images in front of him. Even now, he could barely believe he'd told her he loved her. He'd never told a woman that before. He'd almost told her who he really was, too, and he should have. He'd been kicking himself ever since for losing his nerve....

Still wondering if he'd really seen her, he turned his attention back to the class, moving past the front desks, collecting the votes for the best picture. Once they determined the top three picks, Jimmy figured he'd use their choices to springboard into discussing what made good art.

Sitting on the desk at the front of the room, he began unfolding the papers. When he glanced up, he was surprised to see the students looking so subdued. "For juvenile delinquents," he couldn't help but tease, "you all sure are well behaved."

It was exactly the right thing to say. The room erupted with laughter, breaking the competitive tension. Seeing that, Jimmy wondered if Ches hadn't been right. Maybe he should start looking for an alternative career. If the truth be told, this beat the hell out of drinking with Alex, Benny and Tim.

Besides, Edie Benning would love him better, too.

8

AFTER SETH HAD GONE this morning, Edie's first challenge had come in the form of a call from Pete Shriver, who said Julia was threatening to cancel the wedding and bolt, with or without Lorenzo. Apparently, another photograph taken by the mysterious Jack Stevens had appeared in the *Post*, and while Julia hadn't believed the article—the gist of which was that Lorenzo was seeing another woman—she was saying she couldn't take the pressure any longer.

Neither could Edie. She'd had it up to her eyeballs. Which was why she'd decided to take matters into her own hands.

"C'mon, Jimmy," she muttered now, tucking a folded copy of the *Post* under her arm and sipping a hazelnut latte as she shifted her weight on a metal bench in front of the Puerto Rican Import Company. "I don't have all day." In fact, coming here had only increased her annoyance, since Seth would be coming across town again to meet her soon, and she had plenty of better things to do than ream Jimmy Delaney.

She and Seth had planned to leave for the rehearsal dinner in another two hours, and while it would have been wise to bring him along, there hadn't been time. Besides, Seth had said he needed to do some things around his apartment this morning, so Edie hadn't even mentioned her plan to him. No doubt, he'd have tried to dissuade her, anyway.

"Hurry up," she muttered once more. Seth would be back at her shop in an hour, and she'd called a car service to pick them up, but now she had a flash fantasy that she hadn't really done so, and her heart missed a beat. But no…she distinctly remembered making the arrangements. "You're driving yourself crazy," she whispered in self-censure.

She was always overly organized and a bit on the hypervigilant side, but this morning, her mind was whirring out of control. Reading the *Post* hadn't helped. Taking it from beneath her arm, she stared at the cover again, shaking her head. Once more, Lorenzo was nearly naked in a locker room and talking to an unidentified blonde. According to Pete Shriver, the woman had simply gotten lost and entered the room by mistake. The headline said Julia Jilted? Apparently, Jack Stevens had been up to his old tricks again.

"Who is this guy?" she fumed, still wondering what she was going to say if she found some way to reach him. And would someone who'd stooped to his level listen to her? Probably not, she decided. Still, she'd feel more confident about tonight if she'd at least made her feelings known. That way, whatever happened, she would have warned Delaney she was ready to play hardball. Jack Stevens, too.

According to Pete, his own research hadn't rendered any facts about Jack Stevens, but given Jimmy Delaney's infamy, it stood to reason he'd know everyone in his field. Until moments ago, it hadn't even occurred to her—and maybe not to Pete—to question Jimmy directly. As it turned out, Pete had known where Jimmy was doing his community service. At least he hadn't taken the picture in the paper today. In fact, since being sentenced by Diana Little, he'd seemed to back off, leaving Julia alone. Who knew? Maybe he was actually growing a conscience.

But would he give Edie contact information about Jack, if he had it? Even if he wouldn't, Edie wanted to stare right into Jimmy's eyes—for some strange reason, she imagined they were shimmering green—and hear him say he wouldn't interfere with the party tonight, or the wedding tomorrow. For months, he'd been a thorn in her side, and she wanted two things now: first, to know what he looked like, so she'd recognize him if he showed where he wasn't wanted, and second, to let him know that if she saw hide or hair of him, she'd call the judge, personally.

Tracking down Jimmy had been entirely her own decision, of course, one she'd made after seeing the paper, and Pete Shriver would probably kill her for doing this if he knew, but Edie wasn't about to let anyone show at the last minute in disguise and create a scene. If they did, Julia Darden might snap. And at this point, Jimmy Delaney and Jack Stevens were the only dangling threads that kept needling Edie's consciousness, upsetting her peace of mind.

Emotion twisted inside her as she ran through a mental checklist, the images filling her mind and reminding her, not for the first time, that this really was her own dream wedding. Releasing a breathless sigh, she thought of Seth, and wondered if, somewhere down the road, she might wind up planning another celebration, this time for herself. Smiling, she pushed aside the thought, her mind returning to the business at hand.

Tapping her toe on the concrete to relieve a sudden rush of aggression, she craned to see through the crowd teeming down Bleeker Street. The coffee shop was right across from an old brick walk-up that housed The Little Red Schoolhouse, and when she'd peeked inside and spoken with a security guard, she'd seen the door to Jimmy Delaney's classroom on the first floor, just as she could now, through a window. It was half ajar, and any moment, it would swing fully open, and Jimmy and the kids would come out.

"Hurry up, you cretin," she huffed, glancing at her watch, feeling her hackles rise as she glanced west, in the direction of her shop, almost expecting to see it, although it was six blocks away. After taking another sip of the latte, she exhaled slowly. *Enjoy it,* she thought, savoring the sweet nutty taste. *It'll be your last for the next thirty hours.* She took another steadying breath, whispering, "Thank you," as she gazed at the clear blue sky.

Spring had arrived almost overnight, just in time for Julia's wedding. Now the newscasters had changed their forecast, saying the storm front had moved east, and rain was no longer a probability. People—some locals, some tourists—were milling down the lively street, wearing lightweight jackets and T-shirts, shopping in kiosks brimming with knockoff clothing and handbags. It was hard to believe snow flurries had been in the air only days before. Buckets of flowers were outside all the delis now, and the brightly colored stems blew in the soft breeze.

The Puerto Rican Import Company was heavenly, too, one of Edie's favorite places. Inside, were endless rows of huge barrels, containing imported coffee beans in burlap sacks; she'd started smelling the scent wafting from the open door beside her while she was still a block away. They definitely made a mean latte. Taking another deep swallow, she hoped everything was okay at Big Apple Brides. She'd left a sign on the door, saying she'd gone for lunch, and she'd brought a cell with her, in case anyone needed to reach her. This was going to be her last moment of alone time for the next thirty hours.

And what was she going to say to Jimmy Delaney? Shutting her eyes a moment, she tried to harness her anger, but it was difficult. Between him, Jack Stevens and whoever had started sending Julia the poison-pen letters in October, Edie really feared Julia might do as she'd told Pete this morning—and run. "C'mon, Jimmy." Edie wasn't even sure what he looked like, but she pictured him as good-looking, a real smooth operator.

Blowing out a peeved breath, she opened her eyes and startled. Class must have let out! Inside, the door had swung fully open. Abruptly tossing the remainder of her coffee into the trash bin beside her, she grabbed the newspaper and leaned forward. Kids were spilling down the steps, and now she could see that many had parents waiting for them.

She frowned. At some point, Pete had called Judge Diana Little, who'd told him the kids were offenders whom she felt just needed another outlet, and it must be true, Edie decided now, since they didn't really look like delinquents. Whatever that meant. Wondering if she was being overly judgmental, she realized delinquents probably came in any number of shapes and sizes.

Her heart suddenly palpitated, and she stood. Just on the other side of the door, she now saw the silhouette of a male. As he took long strides toward the outer door, she could see that his head was bent low, as if talking to a tyke too short for Edie to see. She headed across the street, determined to be at the bottom of the steps when he came outside.

She was almost there when he stepped into the sunshine.

Seth? Gasping, she stopped in her tracks. She was close enough to hear the cute little girl next to him squeal, "See you later, Mr. Delaney!"

And then she heard a horn honk. "Get outta the street, lady."

Turning, she fought the urge to offer the cab driver behind her an impassioned Italian gesture. Instead she swung back around and kept moving, even while telling herself to simply turn on her heel once more and head in the opposite direction. Why was Seth on the steps? And why had the girl called him Mr. Delaney?

Because he is, you stupid fool.

Her jaw had slackened, and all the breath seemed to have left her body. Dammit, how could she have been so taken in? Why hadn't she guessed? Of course Jimmy Delaney hadn't given up on shooting the wedding! And it suddenly hurt so much that she gasped, with a soul-wrenching pain she could barely withstand. After all, this wasn't the first time she'd been used, was it? Hadn't Cash Champagne, the man who was now marrying her twin, inserted himself into Edie's life, also, and for the same reason—because he'd wanted to get closer to the Dardens, since Sparky Darden was his father? But that was all water under the bridge....

Bracing her body against panic, she gritted her teeth, willing herself not to feel the pain, but suddenly, all her worst fears assaulted her. For years, she'd grown up with all the old family myths about Miss Marissa's curse, a curse that was uttered on a cold dark February night in the Florida swamps while the Yankees invaded the house where Miss Marissa was to have married Forrest Hartley, her beloved. Granny Ginny had always said that, until the wedding curse was lifted, no Benning woman had a prayer of marrying. But a few weeks ago, when Bridget had come back from Florida, claiming to have ended that chapter of the family history, Edie's heart had leaped with hope.

And then, right after that, when the sexiest man she'd ever met had walked into her life, having so much in common with her, she'd been so sure she'd finally met the love of her life. Emotion knifed sharply inside her. How could he have done this to her? This wasn't about money. This was about her heart. He was such a user...such a taker....

Her eyes met his—not the shimmering green shifty eyes she'd imagined Jimmy Delaney would have, but the hot dark eyes that had trailed over every inch of her while he'd made love to her. Her mind must have short-circuited, because as he came down the steps, he seemed to be moving in slow motion, on the same well-muscled legs that had wrapped around hers, swinging the same long arms that had held her as she'd rocked against him. She tried not to remember how she'd offered her whole self to him, her entire body feeling eaten up with fever.

Meeting her at the bottom of the steps, he lithely leaned and set an artist's portfolio by his feet.

And then Edie raised a hand high and slapped him hard.

JIMMY LET HER HIT HIM. Hell, he deserved it. But why did she have to find out the truth now? Like this? It took all his willpower, but he refrained from any movement, determined not to do what he most wished: close his hand over hers, stop her violent reaction, and then haul her into his arms and kiss her possessively. But he didn't have any such rights. Not anymore.

"Go ahead and hit me again," he found himself saying, vaguely aware that people were breaking stride in the street to watch them, not that they stopped. After all, it was New York.

"I'd like to," she assured, her voice shaking, "but if it's what you want, I'm not about to give you the satisfaction."

"Of course it's not what I want, Edie."

She stared at him a long moment, then simply turned on her heel and headed toward Sixth Avenue. Everything inside him seemed to lurch. He was ready to follow her—his eyes turned hot on her back, his toes flexed in his shoes. He stayed still, though, forcing himself to take a deep breath, trying to pull his thoughts into some logical sequence. It was impossible. One look at her, and he couldn't string two sentences together. All he knew was that he was in love with her.

And that she was leaving him.

"Damn," he muttered. She was so beautiful. Even now, in spite of her clear fury, she was taking away his breath. Her hair was blowing in the spring breeze, cascading around shoulders he'd kissed, naked and bare. Her hair was the color of freshly harvested wheat, catching the sun's rays, and she'd already dressed for the event tonight, in the jersey knit dress she'd ordered online. Of powder blue, it clung to all her curves, accentuating the tuck of her waist and the flare of her hips. *Just let her go, Jimmy.*

She'd gotten his number. Figured him out. Seen

straight through him to the lousy guy he'd become. And she'd just told him what she really thought of him by slapping his face. What was he supposed to do? He could hardly chase her down and tell his side of the story. He didn't have one. Or if he did, it would hardly vindicate him. He'd used her, hoping to get close to her, plain and simple. But then…

He'd fallen for her. Hard and fast. Completely. In a way that had made him feel he was never turning back. She was on the other side of the park now, heading down Bleeker Street. He felt he simply couldn't follow her. He really had no right. And yet he couldn't let her go, either. Abruptly, he started after her, walking at first, then picking his steps up to a jog. She'd just reached the front steps of a church when he caught up to her. From a few feet behind, he breathlessly began, "Look, Edie…"

She whirled around, her usually pale skin flushed, her blue eyes flashing with anger. "I can't believe you followed me."

He threw up his hands. "Me, neither. And I can't say I can explain everything." He raked a hand through his hair, then dropped it to the tie he'd worn with a gray suit, for the dress rehearsal dinner. His fingers, which had rested over the space of his heart, absently squeezed his pectoral, as if that might do something to quell the sense of loss he was starting to feel.

When she turned away once more, something inside him snapped. For a second, he really felt he was losing his mind. She'd come to mean too much to him. He might be in the wrong, but he just couldn't let her go without a fight. Senselessly, he found himself leaning and grabbing her dangling hand, his body moving of its own volition, then he glanced around, noting that people, sensing a lover's quarrel, were starting to stare. Not that he cared what people thought, and yet this was none of their business. "C'mon," he urged, starting up the steps.

Surprisingly she followed, and when they reached the top, she leaned against a stone column near an open door. Just as she did, she hit him again, her fist packing a punch, hurting his shoulder. The fierce anger in her expression said she could pound on him for hours, and that she'd be happy for the release, too. He hated that, as well...hated that he'd provoked her to behavior that didn't suit her. She was so polite, delicate, well mannered. Somehow, he doubted that she'd ever hit anyone before. "Dammit, Edie," he muttered, anyway, angry at the whole situation.

"Me?" she repeated. "Damn *me*? What about you?"

He couldn't stand the wounded sound in her voice. "Dammit," he muttered again, powerless but to reach out and glide his fingers over her shoulder, onto the soft knit fabric of her dress. She was staring at him, slack jawed, her blue eyes open wide and shimmering with tears. She could have been looking at a monster. "Who are you?" she asked rhetorically. Then, "*What* are you?"

"Don't demonize me, Edie," he couldn't help but say, his eyes inadvertently landing on her pouting glossed mouth. He was half tempted to lean closer and capture her lips quickly, before she could protest. He wanted to kiss her so hard and deep that she wouldn't be able to resist, just the way he'd learned she liked it. He wouldn't let go until she was giving in to him, tilting her head back and her hips upward, silently begging for more. He wanted her riding him until they'd reached their release, and to lie in the quiet dark with her, as he had so many nights now, talking and whispering sweet nothings.

Somehow, he was glad it was cooler here, darker and shady. "Don't demonize me," he said again. "I'm not a monster. Just a guy who made a mistake."

"Who walked into my life and…" Stopping herself in midsentence, she nodded her head as if what she was saying was extremely significant and said, "And made a mistake."

"Not you. That's not what I meant."

Ignoring him, she continued, "How did you get the job interview, anyway? Did you pay off people at the headhunting agency? Shouldn't that be illegal?"

Vaguely, he was aware some surrounding pigeons took flight, and glancing behind him, he registered once more that the door to the church was open. That made things worse. He could see icons and statues, an arched vaulted ceiling and grand stained-glass windows. It just added to the travesty of what he'd done. "Something like that," he muttered.

"Not good enough. I want to know exactly what you did," she said, the words coming fast and with venom. "I want to know everything. I want to know how you plotted to weasel into my life. To have sex with me. To use me. Hurt me."

"The references are real," he said, trying to keep his calm, not wanting to let in half of what she'd said. "I've had jobs in art direction—"

"Before you became a slime bag?"

His jaw set. "I thought you said you wanted the truth."

"Is a guy like you even capable of telling it?"

"Old references agreed to back me up if I used a fake

name," he forced himself to continue. "And yeah, I wanted to get some shots of Julia Darden."

Staring into her eyes, he'd never loathed himself more. She'd loved him. He could see it in the foggy depths of her blue irises. It was as if he'd reached deep inside her and simply torn something important and essential right out. His chest felt unbearably tight, and his mind crowded, filling with images of her in bed—how she'd danced for him in the sheer white robe, teasing him until he'd exploded with raw lust.

"But I didn't," he finally added. "I haven't taken any pictures."

Her lips parted further as if she simply couldn't believe his nerve. "Not yet. The wedding's not until tomorrow."

He wasn't used to feeling this hopeless or helpless, and he didn't like it. He felt unbalanced, as if he'd lost the essential center of himself, and was teetering on the edge of some strange abyss he hadn't even known existed until just a moment before. But he didn't want to let her get away. When he spoke, his voice was low and hoarse, barely audible, and if he'd heard it in another context, he never would have recognized it as his own. "I could have taken pictures at any point," he couldn't help but say. "I've been to the Dardens' with you."

"Maybe you did."

Unable to help himself, he came closer, raised a hand and propped it against the column behind her head. She didn't move away, but he wasn't sure that was a good sign. "I didn't, Edie. I swear I didn't."

"We'll never know, will we?"

The column was steadying him, and yet it also further unbalanced him, since he was near enough to smell her freshly washed hair. Apricots and mints knifed to his lungs and he suddenly inhaled even more deeply, drawing in the scent of her as if he'd never have another chance to do so again. "I changed my mind," he said, his dark eyes imploring as he inched his face closer, willing her to look at him deeply, to judge him correctly.

Words were suddenly tumbling from him. "I met you, and then everything changed. I don't care about the pictures. That's not why I've stayed. I…" She was holding her body tightly, and he hated that, too. Dammit, what had he done to her? She'd given herself so openly, so freely, and he'd only hurt her! He dropped a hand to her shoulder, his thumb dipping into the hollow. "I…I'll never forget the promise of meeting your family," he began.

For the briefest instant, he could swear he saw the expression of her eyes soften. "Never forget making love," he continued.

"You've been taking pictures since the wedding was announced in October," she said, her eyes gaining a crafty glint as if she really thought he was just trying to sidetrack her. "And someone's been making attempts on Julia's life. Her *life*. Don't you understand? The woman could die?"

Wincing, briefly shutting his eyes, he opened them only to find he'd come yet another fraction closer. His lips were nearly touching hers, and their breath was mingling. Hers was hotter than the spring breeze on his mouth, teasing him, tempting him, making him ache with need, even as he wondered if she'd ever let him make love to her again. "I didn't know that," he promised. "How could I?"

As she registered the truth, he could see it in her gaze. "The Dardens kept that under wraps," he pressed on.

"It was only when I went out to the estate, and saw Julia fighting with Pete and Lorenzo that I realized how serious it was…."

Her tone was sharp, the lost trust in her eyes the most cutting thing he'd ever felt. For a second, he simply felt those eyes searing into him. They burned. Cut like a razor. But at least she was still standing here. At least she was still talking to him. "You didn't get the seriousness of it?"

When he nodded, she shook her head ruefully, and when she spoke again, her voice came out sounding strangled. "What? You don't think what you do affects lives?"

She was going too far now. "I didn't send those letters, Edie." His eyes pierced hers. "And hell yes," he added. "I know what I do affects people."

"Princess Diana died when a guy like you decided he wanted—"

"A picture? Maybe. But I don't play the game that way. I never did. I never endangered Julia's life."

"No." She shook her head adamantly. "You only contributed to a bad situation, making it worse."

"For a while by taking pictures, not lately."

"Who's Jack Stevens?"

He raised an eyebrow. "Oh," he suddenly said, not understanding the segue at first. "That's why you're here. You found out where Jimmy Delaney was working from Pete Shriver," he guessed. "And you wanted to find Jack and tell him off."

"You, too. I wanted to make sure you didn't show at the wedding."

"I'll do whatever you want, Edie."

"Who is he?"

He lifted a shoulder, shrugging, half-glad they'd shifted topics. Maybe it boded well. "I don't know. I asked around."

She looked appalled. "Oh, no. And you're Vinny Marcel. I almost forgot. Hmm. About trying to find Jack Stevens—I'll bet you didn't do so for Julia's sake." Guilt must have shown in his features, since she blew out a sound of frustration and shook her head in disgust. "I knew it."

"I was curious," he said simply.

"Afraid someone with more talent than you for invading people's privacy finally hit the scene?"

"Something like that," he said again.

She suddenly gasped. "That's why you were defending the paparazzi the night we went to Hunan Pan."

He couldn't help but say, his voice almost breaking, "The first night we made love."

That seemed to strike a nerve. Color drained from her flushed cheeks, and she licked at lips that had apparently gone dry. Her eyes shifted away from his, and suddenly, she looked as if she'd rather be anywhere else in the world but here. It was the wrong time to mention that a car was coming soon to take both of them to the Dardens', so he didn't.

Wincing once more, he felt as if something inside him had opened like a trapdoor. Any self-respect he had left was now falling through the hole. "You still think about that night…." he murmured, willing her to do so.

"Don't remind me," she whispered.

It was too much. His hands were on her face, stroking her cheeks, then in her hair. "You don't want to forget our first time together," he whispered, not daring to kiss her, although he wanted to desperately. "I know I don't. I never will, Edie."

Splaying his fingers, he fanned them near her temple, then pushed them upward, into silken strands before making a light fist against her scalp.

"Look, Edie," he began. "I know it's lame, but…" Pausing, he sighed. "When I first started taking pictures, my Mom was sick. My Dad…well, he owns a little hardware shop in Ohio. He's self-employed and not the best with details. He'd let the insurance lapse. And then my mother got cancer."

He searched her eyes, half hating himself for bringing this up now, knowing he was asking her to forgive him. Still, he felt he was using his family sob story to justify himself, and yet that's not really how he meant it. Or maybe it was. Whatever the case, he wanted her to know him better, to understand him.

But he felt so confused every time he looked into her eyes. Tied up in knots. As if he was about to lose the only thing he'd ever felt was important outside his immediate family…a woman he hadn't even known just fifteen days ago.

"She's okay now," he went on. "The cancer's in remission. But…she had both breasts removed. Chemo. Some complications. And more than a few hospital stays. We couldn't get insurance by then. She had preexisting conditions, and at the time, I was just finishing up art school at NYU. My résumé isn't fake, and I really did work at those jobs, like I said."

He swallowed hard. "I was going back and forth to Ohio all the time. That was expensive, too. But my Dad was all alone, and without my Mom, he's lost. He's one of those guys who only looks like he's ruling the roost. All bark and no bite. A real tough guy, as long as she's beside him. Without her around, the guy can barely dress himself, much less cook his own breakfast...."

He'd let his voice trail off, and now, he felt if he began to speak again, it would break. His father was strangely vulnerable, and yet so externally tough, the kind of guy who'd been born and bred long before the feminism of the seventies, or male encounter groups that had started trying to tell guys it was okay to have feelings. And Jimmy Delaney loved his old man with a passion. His mother, too. Somehow, he hoped Edie would hear it in his voice...would understand. "He felt so bad about what happened. Felt it was his fault that Mom didn't have insurance and we couldn't cover the bills. And...well, it was his fault. But I couldn't stand watching him blame himself. He really couldn't cut himself a break."

He took a deep breath, then plunged on. "When she first got sick—a lot of it's kind of a blur now—my dad and I were at the hospital, watching TV. Shows I'd never really watched, like *Jeopardy.* And all the tabloid shows like *Entertainment Tonight.* I guess that registered. I sort of remember wondering how much money those guys made for the pictures they took...and then a few weeks later, when I came back to the city, I stopped in the Suds Bar over by my place. It's on Avenue A. My place is over on B. The way things worked out, I ran into these three guys who were actually taking celebrity photographs, and doing better than just paying their rent. We wound up having some beers...."

She didn't look as if she even believed him, but every word was true. "Alex, Benny and Tim." He forced himself to continue, despite the disbelief in her expression. He shook his head, remembering, wishing, he guessed, for some detail that would somehow touch her, and make her realize he hadn't always been what she'd called him...a slime bag. "They showed me the ropes," he managed to say. "Where to find the celebs. How to get on the party lists. Who to sell to and for how much. How to play buyers off each other."

"You've been doing this awhile, Seth—" She stopped herself, and looked suddenly stricken. Maybe she was remembering, as he was, how many times she'd cried that name in the darkness. Now he could hear her voice playing in his ears like a music he'd never hear again, raining down soft whimpers that touched his shoulders like the kisses from her lips. *Seth...Seth.*

Suddenly, he couldn't take the tension of this any longer. He had to fight not to give up. To simply turn around and head in the opposite direction. Or maybe go inside the church and just rail at God and ask what he'd done that was so wrong. And yet he knew. Ches was right. So was Edie. "I walked out on my life," he admitted, a thread of anger creeping into his tone. "My talent. You don't think I know that?" Taking a deep breath, he blew it out all at once, shaking his head, barely able to believe what he'd been doing with his time.

"Whole years seem like a dream now," he muttered, willing her to understand. For at least two of them he'd gone from city to city, like a bat out of hell, not knowing which was more difficult, caring for his father or mother. All the while, the bills had been piling up. But he'd gotten on the circuit and it had paid off. Medical expenses that had been staggering were something he, Jimmy Delaney, could simply write a check for. Because he hadn't grown up with much, and because he'd shown an early talent for art, he'd never expected to see the kind of money that began to move through his hands. Dollars had wound up spilling through his fingers like water.

"A dream," he repeated. A blur of hospital rooms. So many of the memories looked exactly like the photographs he'd taken during that time. They were sad pictures…pictures he couldn't stand to look at now. They haunted him. All were pictures of death and grief…yellow-looking hallways lined with gurneys gleaming under fluorescent lights. Grim-faced nurses. His once powerful dad looking grossly haggard. The woman he most loved smiling as she wasted away.

But he'd saved her. And yet he knew that wasn't strictly true, either. Call it what you will, God or Fate, but when it came to life and death, even Jimmy Delaney knew he had no real power.

"Maybe the rush of it got to me in the end," he said. "I don't know. After she got better, I'd been in the game for a while. I had a reputation I'd been too busy to even know I'd gotten. And I wanted the money. It was more than that, though. I got into the rush. The scam of trying to take the hard-to-get pictures." He sighed. "It didn't make me happy," he found himself admitting, even though he doubted she cared anymore. "I blew a lot of the money on fancy vacations and women who didn't matter…."

And, somehow, even though he knew he'd lost Edie, it felt good to say it all. Feeling his eyes sting, he abruptly glanced away, pulling his hands from her shoulders, putting them on his hips. Even now, he didn't really understand any of it. He just knew he'd gotten lost, somehow. He'd felt as though he was day-tripping through his own life, not really living it. It was as if someone else's life had come along and swept him away, taking him too far from his roots, his dreams and his source. And only Edie had pulled him back.

He shook his head. "I think...after my mother got better...maybe it was the relief that kept me flying high. Or the fear that came in the wake of realizing my folks weren't going to be around forever. That I had no brothers and sisters. And that I was going to be alone in the world. Ches had married Elsa and was never around." Pausing, he managed to close his mouth. He'd said too much, anyway. He'd always been so damn artistic for a guy, too emotional. Passionate. He shook his head again. Swallowed hard.

And then he simply said, "I'm sorry. Really sorry, Edie. I swear I am."

She looked torn. "I don't know what to believe."

He'd lied too much to be believed. "I know you don't."

"I have to go," she said finally, the words both simple and crushing.

Somehow, he managed to nod. He sure as hell didn't blame her. He'd leave, too. As she turned and started down the steps, he pressed a knuckle to his lips, knowing it was over. And yet he couldn't hold back the words. "Edie?"

She turned and now he could see tears in her eyes. "Yes?"

"I love you."

She looked at him a long moment and said, "You already told me that."

"I wasn't lying when I said it," he managed.

But she only turned once more and walked away.

9

"MR. DELANEY?"

The vision of watching Edie walk away had become too much for him, so Jimmy had sat on the church steps and shut his eyes briefly, bracing himself against unwanted emotion. He felt as if there were a hollowed-out void where his heart used to be.

"Are you okay, Mr. Delaney?"

He recognized Melissa Jones's voice before he opened his eyes. Staring at the little girl, he took a deep breath, still wondering how to handle what had transpired with Edie, forcing himself not to look west down Bleeker Street in her direction, thinking he couldn't stand to see her again right now. He tilted his lips encouragingly, but was powerless to make the smile meet his eyes. Melissa was as cute as a button, standing there dressed in an outfit that made her look as if she could have been a pint-size rock-and-roll star at Woodstock—wearing low-slung jeans and a fringe-hemmed jacket. Countless strands of beads looped around her neck. More were gathered around the bottom of dark pigtails that almost touched her shoulders.

"Oh, my portfolio," he murmured, his mind still mulling over the fight. He stared at the case that Melissa had hauled across the street, then leaned and took it from her. Its handle came up to her waist, and for her, it had probably been heavy.

"You left it on the steps."

"Sorry. I—" *Was chasing my girlfriend.* Lover, he mentally amended. Or more likely, past lover. Chewing his lower lip, he tried to tamp down a rush of self-loathing. He'd really blown it with Edie.

"No problem, Mr. Delaney."

"Thank you," he managed to say, kicking himself for having left the case, since that had meant, in turn, one of his students had wound up following him. Worse, judging by the look on Melissa's face, she'd heard everything. And she was only about eleven. Racking his brain, he tried to remember all the details of what he'd said to Edie. Had he used foul language? Cursed? How explicit had he been about what they'd done in bed? He frowned. "Didn't your parents pick you up?"

Shrugging, she plopped down beside him, careful to put a protective hand over the camera slung around her neck. "Nope. I'm s'posed to take a cab home."

"Where do you live?"

"Uptown. Harlem."

He tried not to react visibly. But wasn't she a little young to be running around Manhattan by herself? Unfortunately, she seemed to read his mind. "It's just a cab," she assured defensively. "I take them by myself all the time. And my parents gave me a cell phone. The cabbie's not exactly going to drive off with me."

Probably true. He glanced away, his eyes now searching for Edie in the crowds, only to have his attention pulled suddenly back to Melissa when she slipped one of her hands over his. Surprised, he instinctively gave her fingers a squeeze. The little girl's dark eyes captured his, and she blinked at him a few times in quick succession, her whole face screwing up in a way that was incredibly endearing—the corners of her eyes wrinkled, her ears wiggled and her lips squinched into a crinkled dot. Opening her eyes, she squeezed his hand once more. "I couldn't help but hear everything," she said. "I didn't mean to, but I just thought you forgot your portfolio...."

"It's okay," he assured.

"No, it's not, Mr. Delaney," she said, wincing. Gritting her teeth, she then made a soft clucking sound before racing on. "Just like you, I got into a lot of trouble, too," she admitted. "So, I know how it feels. I like to shop." Shaking her head, she shot him a sheepish glance. "I maxed out my mom's credit cards, then I got caught shoplifting at Bloomingdale's."

He'd been wondering what such a cute kid could have done wrong. He studied her. "You're a junior shopaholic?"

"Kleptomaniac," she corrected. "That's what my dad said."

"Why did you do it?"

She shook her head. "Maybe because my parents stay so busy. They go out most nights, and usually this lady, Mrs. Rodriguez, comes over. She likes to watch TV." Suddenly looking away, she interrupted herself and shifted topics. "That was the woman who's planning Julia Darden's wedding, right?"

"Yeah." He blew out a sigh. "It's tomorrow at three."

"And tonight's something..."

He could hardly believe he was telling his problems to an eleven-year-old, but he really needed to talk to someone. Anyone. Right now, he was fighting not to simply run after Edie, but she'd made her position clear.

Probably, if he chased her, he'd make things worse. "The rehearsal dinner's at five," he muttered, thinking out loud. "Afterward, from eight to eleven, there's a party."

That seemed to pique her interest. "At the estate?"

He nodded.

"It's in Long Island, right?"

He named the town.

Melissa looked away a long moment. "I saw those pictures in the paper by Jack Stevens."

"Some of my buddies actually thought I took them," he said, "but I didn't."

"And she doesn't believe you weren't going to take pictures at the wedding?"

Melissa was referring to Edie. "No. I don't think so."

Withdrawing her hand, she crossed her hands over her chest. "She wants to know who Jack Stevens is?"

"Yeah. That's why she came over here."

She sighed. "Yeah..." she repeated. "I saw those pictures in the *Post*. They were pretty good, huh?"

He frowned. "You shouldn't read the tabloids."

"Then you shouldn't sell pictures to them."

A good point. "I haven't lately," he defended.

"Only started working with the wedding planner, right?"

Puffing his cheeks to blow, he exhaled another long breath. "I was going to use her," he admitted. "I wanted to get close enough to crash the wedding."

"That's a good idea."

He shot her a sideways glance. "Hmm. I thought you'd given up a life of crime."

She giggled. "I never said that."

He rolled his eyes. "You're too young to start ruining your life."

"I'll have time for that later on, huh?"

"I didn't start until my teens," he assured.

"But I don't want to be bored for the next five years."

"You're a tough nut to crack," he said.

She smiled up at him, and his heart lifted. Just looking at her made hope surge inside him. He'd bet Melissa Jones had that effect on a lot of people. Her eyes were always sparkling, bespeaking a mischievous quality, and yet she was paradoxically sincere. *Kids are so great*, he thought, his heart swelling. Just moments ago, he'd been fantasizing about a future with Edie, a family. Now he was sure his own deceit had closed the door on what could have been a great life.

The emotion in Melissa's face was so transparent, and her eyes were shining with concern. He thought he saw something else that looked strangely like guilt. But what, beyond her own childish transgressions, could Melissa Jones have done to make her feel guilty?

She said, "Do you want to marry her?"

Fat chance now. "To tell you the truth, I was thinking along those lines, Melissa."

She squeezed her eyes shut, making her face pucker, so it looked almost as if her nose was being suctioned through a vacuum. "Then go get her, tiger," she said, suddenly opening her eyes and punching his arm.

He couldn't help but chuckle at her encouragement. "I don't think she's going to take me back."

"You won't know until you try."

Maybe she was right. He was sure Edie would refuse to see him. But then, this was Edie. *Edie*, he thought again. No…he couldn't just let go. "I'd better put you in a cab first."

"Okay," Melissa agreed.

Lifting his portfolio in one hand and taking Melissa's in the other, he stood. "Are you sure you're okay to head uptown by yourself?"

"In a cab? Sure."

Deciding she was probably right, he lifted an arm to hail a taxi, and one pulled to the curb immediately. "There you go. Get in. And oh—"

Climbing inside, she looked at him through the rolled-down window as he slammed the door. "Hmm?"

"Congratulations on winning best picture in class."

She beamed. "Thanks."

He'd been surprised. He'd figured the kids would chose some of the campier, funnier shots. But they'd gone for the one that had communicated the most heart and complexity. Never underestimate kids, he thought. They might be delinquents, but they'd gone for the gold. "Have a good ride home," he added.

Her voice hitched. "You really think I'm good?"

He spoke honestly. "I think you could be great, Melissa. You captured something special in the picture of your parents." Like all budding artists, she was seeing things beyond her years, things she probably couldn't describe in words, but only in images.

"The pictures of the homeless man were really something, too." She'd taken a series of pictures of some bum in her neighborhood who'd apparently been getting on his feet. In the first shots, the man had looked unwashed and ragged. Not like he'd been on the streets long, but haggard, with a scraggly beard, unkempt clothes and the hope gone from his eyes. "What happened to him?" he couldn't help but ask, thinking of how the pictures showed the man's amazing transformation, seemingly over the past few weeks. The light had come back into his blue eyes. He'd gotten a haircut and new clothes, maybe at a shelter.

"What do you think happened?" Melissa asked rhetorically. "He met me!" She laughed. "And when I saw him sleeping below my fire escape, I took him dinner. He said the shelter was too noisy and he couldn't think straight."

As she plunged on, talking about her relationship with the homeless man on her block, Jimmy felt a twinge of concern. "Do your folks know about this friendship, Melissa?"

She rolled her eyes, her mouth slackening in pique as if she'd expected far more understanding from the likes of Jimmy Delaney. "Of course not!" Now looking angrily at him, she said to the driver, "C'mon. We'd better go."

Jimmy patted the side of the taxi and it took off. Only then did he shake his head and whisper, "She's redeemed some homeless man." If this was Melissa Jones at eleven, he pitied the man who'd meet her when she was eighteen. Pressing a hand to his eyes, he chuckled softly. "Too much," he whispered.

So was his situation with Edie. In about an hour, he was to have been in a car with her, heading to the estate. She needed his help, too. But he couldn't think of a way to get back in her good graces, short of figuring out where Jack Stevens was and wresting a promise from the man that he wouldn't crash Julia Darden's wedding. Oh, yeah. Maybe he could unmask the perpetrator who'd been sending Julia the threatening letters since October, too. Teams were really sizing up players, right now, and just yesterday, Edie had said all the unwanted attention was affecting Lorenzo's concentration. He hadn't played well this year.

Hmm. Suddenly, Jimmy wondered if Julia wasn't the real target of the threatening letters. According to Edie, Pete had said he thought it possible an old business rival of Sparky Darden's was sending the letters, hoping to hurt Julia's father by ruining his daughter's wedding, since it was so important to him. Pete had said the perpetrator wanted to keep people on edge, afraid and tense. But what if the target was Lorenzo? Jimmy wondered. Not Julia, nor her father? "Who knows," Jimmy muttered.

And anyway, he had more pressing troubles on his mind, besides solving the many mysteries surrounding the Darden wedding. Gripping a hand more tightly around the handle of his portfolio, he started walking west, toward Big Apple Brides...and Edie.

It was a fool's mission, but he'd never forgive himself if he didn't try.

As she continued barreling across town, Edie felt as if she'd left her own body, somehow. Where her mind really was, she couldn't say—floating above her somewhere, or trailing behind. Either way, she felt as if she was moving through a thick fog. As she passed Sheridan Square, then headed down Christopher Street and hit Hudson, she fought the urge to look over her shoulder, telling herself she didn't care if Jimmy was following her. She didn't really *want* him to follow her, she vowed. She wanted...

To turn the clock back an hour, to when she was staring into her bedroom mirror, turning this way, then that, admiring how the new powder-blue dress fit, hugging her body in all the right places. She'd been imagining how Seth's eyes were going to light up when he saw it.

No doubt, she'd been thinking, he'd glide his warm palms over her hips while kissing her deeply, possessively, sliding his tongue between her lips, getting them both so hot and bothered that they'd feel desperate to make love, even though they'd have to stop because they were to leave for the Dardens'. She'd assumed she and Seth would keep tossing kindling on the fire throughout the night—sharing surreptitious touches and stolen kisses that would burn in her belly, making her ready for a wild night that was to come.

But Seth wasn't even his name.

Relief flooded her when the shop came into sight, and she shook her head in stunned bewilderment. Just an hour ago, she'd been living a fantasy beyond her heart's most secret dreams. The wedding would be beautiful, she'd been coaching herself, and despite all the problems of the past few months—everything from the announcement about the Benning wedding curse on *Rate the Dates*, to the mysterious arrival of Jack Stevens on the scene—Edie knew she'd planned the best possible wedding. After tonight's party, she'd expected that she and the man she'd been calling Seth would unwind together, make love and say those precious words to each other again, *I love you.*

Right now, she'd give anything to be living that fantasy still. Just for another hour. A day. At least until the wedding was over. Why had she made the fatal error of crossing town to confront Jimmy Delaney? And what if she hadn't? Would Seth have told her who he was? Or would he have taken pictures at the wedding? Had that been his real plan—to use her, take the pictures, then leave her? Was he lying about how his feelings had changed?

Reaching the entrance of Big Apple Brides, she un-
locked the front door and headed for the desk, tears
pressing at her eyelids, making them feel swollen. "You
can't cry," she muttered. She'd already put on eye
shadow and mascara. And the car would be here soon.
She still had a job to do. This might be Julia's big day,
but it was just as important for Edie, since its success
could help her business to flourish. Staring at the windows of her own shop, she felt her heart suddenly
wrench in her chest as her eyes trailed over the display
items—the champagne glasses, hope chest, garters and
bouquets. Her throat constricted as she took in the
winged mannequin wearing the gown of white feathers, surrounded by roses.

Then she realized her heart was still hammering too
hard in her chest, and she felt light-headed. Dammit,
why did this man have such an effect on her? She'd do
anything she could to tamp down the racing of her
heart, the dizzy feeling in her blood as she recalled the
scent of his cologne. Would she never feel him in her
arms again? Never feel excitement dance along all her
nerve endings when his mouth claimed hers?

Behind her, she heard the door open, and she whirled
around. Everything inside her froze when she saw him
lean, set his portfolio case beside the door, kick the door
shut, then stride toward her. Reaching, he touched the
sleeve of her dress lightly, tracing the fabric with his finger. "Look," he murmured, his voice raspy and catching. "Can't we talk about this some more…."

Her lips parted in astonishment, and the pain she'd
initially felt on acknowledging his betrayal ripped
through her again. "And make up?" she managed to
say. "Of course we can't. You used me…." Pausing, she

swallowed hard and said his name. "Jimmy." Sucking in a quick breath, she added, "I can barely say your name. I'm used to calling you Seth. But I don't know who you really are, not really." When he only stepped closer, she wished she hadn't reopened the conversation at all. She should have known better. This could lead absolutely nowhere.

"Yes, you do," he coaxed, his dark eyes willing her to reconsider, to try to understand his position. "I'm the man you've been making love to for the past two weeks. That hasn't changed, Edie."

"Oh, yes, it has," she forced herself to say, her eyes flitting to the door and seeing a dark sedan glide in front of it. As she waved, the driver got out, letting the engine idle, clearly ready to open the back door for her whenever she came outside. She stared at Jimmy, taking in the nice suit, neatly cut dark hair, his clean-shaven jaw. An hour ago, he would have conjured up old-fashioned words such as dashing. Now he just looked dishonest and slick.

"I was making love to a figment," she insisted, her heart swelling, feeling as if it might burst from the truth of what she was saying. "A no one. A figment of your imagination. Some guy named Seth Bishop who doesn't even exist."

"I exist, Edie," he said, his voice too low and hoarse, too seductive. His hand was on her now, his long fingers curling around her upper arm, pulling her closer; almost against her will, she felt her feet stumbling toward him. She was a moth to the flame. Metal to a magnet. And now that she'd had a taste of him, she wondered if she'd ever really be free again.

"Stop," she said simply.

"No," he returned, now leaning so sweet, heavenly breath hit her lips, flooding her body with pure fire that she was powerless to resist. "You know I can't stop," he persisted, his voice ragged, that breath still feathering on her lips. "Not after what we've discovered about each other. You're right for me. We belong together. Isn't that what we've been saying?"

"I belonged with some man named Seth Bishop."

"I'm him."

"You're Jimmy," she muttered, shaking off his grasp. She started to step backward, then realized the desk was behind her and there was nowhere to go. "Jimmy Delaney." Her eyes found his once more, and she stared deeply into the dark depths, her lips parting, since she really couldn't believe how little he cared. How could he have done this? "Why did you come here? I've got a rehearsal dinner. Now. Not next week or next month. Now. I've worked years to wind up running my own business. Months on what's going to happen over the next twenty-four hours. If you cared about me, you'd never have done this—"

"I didn't know," he shot back, edging closer, pinning her with the hard muscles of his long legs, making her shudder with a response she'd rather die than feel right now. His voice dropped another husky notch. "When I applied for the job, I knew you were attractive. I'd seen you before. But I had no idea I'd..."

Fall in love with you.

She tried not to hear the words hanging in the air. "This is an opportunity for me."

"And I don't want to blow it for you, Edie."

"Then leave."

"Didn't anything I said get through to you?"

"I believe you got into the business of shooting celebrity photographs with good intentions," she forced herself to say, and that much was true. "And I'm glad your mother's better." That was true, also. "But you stayed in the business, as well. Long after you needed to. You had other dreams, but you walked away. And maybe that says something about your character."

"I'm changing. You changed me, Edie."

"Wanting to use me is what led you to my doorstep, Jimmy." She paused. "And right now, I guess it's what led you back."

"You led me back."

He leaned quickly then, his lips nearly brushing hers. They hovered a breath away. With him this close, she felt as if a rug had been pulled out from under her feet. Truly, he was too close for comfort. She couldn't think now. A hair couldn't pass between them, and his lips...she felt them on hers—soft and hot, trembling and greedy, now touching in what wasn't quite a kiss.

It was more than she could take. Her knees weakened. Her willpower vanished. And while she damned her own body for its traitorous response, it was no use. He'd loved every inch of her. They'd lain in bed naked together, their bodies burning. She couldn't forget...she'd never forget....

Even now, she wanted him. One touch, and she feared she might say to hell with the wedding that meant so much to her. She wanted to grab his hand, take him upstairs, strip for him again. She wanted to slowly remove his clothes, tongue every inch of his skin and watch him beg her for more. Fury was bubbling inside her, and she wanted to feel her power over him....

Dammit, what had she done? Outside, the driver honked the car's horn. She could tell Jimmy to get away from her. Somehow, she'd field the Darden wedding, herself. Her parents and sisters would be there, after all. And so many of the other workers were responsible and competent. No, she didn't need him. Her cell phone rang, and she brought it to her ear, snapping the on button.

"Paulie," the voice said.

"Paulie," she managed. "What's up?"

"I hate to tell you this, but we've got a problem."

She could hear countless voices in the background, the sound of instruments as musicians warmed up. "What's wrong?"

"It'll wait until you get here, but we're confused about the arrangement of some of the flowers."

"I'm on my way," she managed, thinking she was probably going to need every hand she could get. "Okay," she found herself saying as she turned off the phone.

The man in front of her looked so hopeful, it nearly broke her heart. "Okay...?"

"You can come with me. Just get in the car." Brushing past him, she headed for the door. "And Se—Jimmy?"

"Yeah?"

Her blue eyes lasered into his, sharply focusing, as if she could stare straight through him, and read his deepest, most hidden motivations. "You swear you're not going to take any pictures?"

"No. I wasn't going to, Edie."

She wanted to believe him, but she suspected it was a mistake. "Don't," she said simply.

"I won't."

"Well, if you're coming," she found herself saying abruptly, hardly wanting to examine her own motivations too deeply for acting against her own best judgment, "you can bring all the files on the corner of the desk."

10

"STAY IN MY HAIR," Melissa demanded insistently, wincing as she accidently poked her head with a bobby pin again. Trying once more, she skewered her hair, pulling it to the side, away from her temple. Stepping back, she looked at herself in the bedroom mirror, then shrugged.

She guessed she looked okay. The white, daisy-printed dress was calf length, and she was wearing it with her new white leggings and patent leather shoes. She'd had difficulty reaching behind herself, but she'd tied the long yellow sash as well as she could. Maybe the driver of the car she'd ordered could retie it for her. After she'd phoned a car service, she'd borrowed some cash from a glass jar, the one in which her father always emptied his pockets after work, which meant she could tip well enough for a favor.

Still frowning at the sloppy bow, she muttered, "Forget it. Just hurry." Her mother had chosen the outfit, and it was supposed to be for Easter—her grandparents were coming in from Yonkers to visit and they were going to church at Saint John the Divine, where her parents knew the minister—so Melissa felt a little guilty about wearing it. Still, even if the bow was messed up, the dress seemed like something she'd be expected to wear to a rehearsal for a bride.

Her parents had left for the party about twenty minutes ago. All night, in preparation for sneaking out, Melissa had been pretending to be sick. Now she crossed to the canopy bed she'd begged her parents to buy for her tenth birthday, and she drew back the covers, checking the pillows she'd arranged beneath to simulate the form of her sleeping body.

"Super," she whispered. Carefully, she drew up the covers once more, tucking them around the dark-haired head of a doll. Glancing around, she wondered if there was anything she'd forgotten, then suddenly gasped. "The lightbulb!" Gently, she removed it from the bedside lamp, just in case Mrs. Rodriguez came into the room and tried to turn on the light.

Not that she would, Melissa decided, slipping the bulb under the bed. Tiptoeing to the door, she opened it a crack and stared toward the den. "Super," she whispered once more. Everything was moving along, right on schedule.

Mrs. Rodriguez was watching TV. If her parents called to check on Melissa, Mrs. Rodriguez would say she was asleep. Later, of course, her parents would realize she hadn't been sick, nor in bed, but Melissa would cross that bridge when she came to it. Feeling sure she heard movements outside, she backed slowly from the door until she'd reached the fire-escape window.

She lifted one of her mother's pocketbooks from the sill and opened it, making sure she'd placed her camera and cell phone inside. She wished she had a zoom lens. And that she could take a flash, but she'd figured high-speed film would work. That way, she wouldn't draw attention to herself when she used the camera.

"All systems go." She had the invitation, too. It was

on heavy, cream-colored stock, addressed to her parents. Because her father was an important sportscaster, he knew Lorenzo Santini really well. Which was, of course, how Melissa had gotten into the locker room to take pictures of Lorenzo. Just thinking of it, made her cheeks warm. Before Lorenzo, she'd never seen a man so close to nude. Really, each time she'd shot him he'd had something—a towel or a bunched wad of clothes—in front of him, but the newspapers had made it look as if he'd been completely naked.

"Here goes," she whispered. Very carefully, wincing every time it creaked, Melissa pulled back the heavy gate in front of the window. Already, she'd lifted the window, and now she climbed through and pulled the gate into place again. Then she glanced down two flights to the street. "So super," she whispered excitedly. Jack was pulling down the bottom of the fire-escape ladder for her. Waving, she scrambled downward, determined to get to the bottom before the car service arrived. "Hey," she said grinning once she'd reached the bottom. This was what her mom called synchronicity.

"Are you sure this is a good idea?" asked Jack.

"It's super-duper," she assured as she grabbed his arm and pulled him around the building to the front where the car would be waiting. "And you look great."

It was an understatement. A few weeks ago, Jack had looked hopeless and helpless, like a poster man for grim advertisements in the subway that asked for donations for the homeless. When she'd first discovered him and had started feeding him, he'd been sleeping on a sheet of cardboard beneath the back fire escape she'd just scrambled down. Now he was a changed man. He was showered and clean shaven, wearing new jeans, a freshly pressed shirt and a sport coat. A duffel bag full of new clothes was slung over his shoulder.

Over the past few weeks, after opening the bank account for her, he'd continued working as her middleman, selling pictures to the press, at least one per day, and now he'd used his share of the money, just as he'd said he would, to start a self-improvement program. He'd sworn he'd been at rock bottom, without hope of anything good coming his way that could turn his life around, but then, suddenly, he'd said Melissa had appeared in his life like an angel, and now he had a second chance. A new lease on life, he'd called it.

"There's the car," she said, rounding the corner. She pointed. "It's way up at the other end of the block, see?"

His jaw slackened, and he raked a hand through his short auburn hair. "You called a limo?"

"Just a car. They must not have had the other kind."

"Other kind?" he repeated. "You mean a sedan?"

"What's a sedan, Jack?"

"A regular car."

"Yeah. They musta just had this stretch limo."

He sighed once more, as if to say all this had somehow gotten far beyond his control. "Are you sure you want to go out to this party in Long Island? Are you telling me the truth about your parents being there?"

Melissa smiled at him sweetly. "Would I lie?"

"Yes," Jack said flatly.

She nodded. "Well, I'm not lying this time. I just want to be with my parents tonight. You know, how I told you they go out and leave me at home? Well, I want to surprise them." And she wasn't sure she had enough money for her horse. Pictures of the Darden rehearsal dinner would be worth a tidy sum, and if she finagled an invitation to the wedding tomorrow, she'd have enough to hang up her photography career.

At the thought, Melissa felt a twinge of disappointment. After all, Jimmy Delaney had said she was good, and she was pretty sure he'd meant it. She blew out a sigh. She could sure use Jack's help after tonight, since she wasn't sure how to sell the pictures by herself. Still, she didn't want to discourage Jack from checking himself into the rehab center because he really needed to go. Regarding how to sell whatever pictures she took, she decided she'd cross that bridge later.

"Now, Melissa," Jack Stevens said, slipping a checkbook from the inner pocket of his coat. "You take this. And I want you to listen to me."

She turned her full attention to him, suddenly feeling excitement course through her veins. She couldn't believe she was actually crashing Julia Darden and Lorenzo Santini's party. Probably, it was for grown-ups and she'd be the only kid there. Too bad her dreamy teacher, Jimmy Delaney, wasn't going to be there, as well. But given how things had gone with Edie Benning, that seemed unlikely.

And better for Melissa. Guilty heat crept into her cheeks. After all, she knew very well who Jack Stevens was—he was sitting right next to her!—and even though Jimmy had wrongly inserted himself into his girlfriend's life, she couldn't help but feel she was somewhat responsible for his troubles. Suddenly realizing Jack had been talking to her, she said, "Hmm?"

He blew out a frustrated sigh. "I asked you to listen to me, sweetheart."

"I am," she promised.

"I really appreciate your help," he began, looking

torn. "I mean it. But what we've done is...well, probably not exactly illegal. Still, it's wrong, Melissa. If I wasn't in such a jam, I'd never have agreed to help you...."

Opening the clasp of her mother's pocketbook, she dropped the checkbook inside. "I know," she said. "But aren't you happy you did?"

He took another breath, as if he wasn't quite sure what to say. "In a way," he finally said. "I admit it, Melissa. I don't know...I guess I'd given up hope. I was doing more than just eating in soup kitchens. I was getting the whole routine down, learning where to go for the best meals, where to pick up food stamps, finding out which shelters were the safest to sleep in. I was well on my way to just accepting my fate, and making that my lifestyle."

She waited expectantly, wondering why he was going into all this again. He'd only been homeless for about a month, and he'd been staying at the men's shelter a few blocks away when he'd said the noise inside had driven him into the night. She'd discovered him almost immediately, downing a pint of what he'd called liquid comfort while curled up beneath her fire escape. Now she felt confused. "So, everything's super, right?"

He knelt down in front of her, just as the dark limousine glided in front of the building, and the driver got out, circled it and opened a back door. "I know you've been real kind to me, sweetheart," he said. "And I know you want that horse real bad. But you can't keep going around talking to homeless men. And before we part company, I want your word you won't ever do it again. If I have any sense that you will, I'm going to do my twenty-eight days in rehab, then get out and come talk to your parents. I'm worried about you, Melissa Jones."

She could feel her face fall. Her throat was suddenly tight and dry, and she found it difficult to swallow around a lump. "But this turned out super," she protested. "I thought you really liked me."

"I do."

"Well, then why are you mad at me?"

"I'm not mad. And things did turn out super," he agreed. "But not every homeless man might be as nice as me. I mean, I'm a guy going through a rough time. No doubt about it. But now, I want my wife and son back, and…" He heaved a sigh. "And you're responsible for…for touching my heart. You're so sweet. Such a nice kid. Just having you bring me leftovers from your family dinners restored some hope in me. I won't deny that. But that's exactly why I'm so worried about you.…"

Like most adults, Jack Stevens was turning out to be crazy. Melissa could only shake her head. Jimmy Delaney was pretending to be a man named Seth Bishop, and he'd weaseled his way into the Darden wedding by cozying up to a wedding planner. And Melissa's parents worked so hard, always saying they had to set an example and be pillars of the community, but they never had time to enjoy anything at all. Which made Melissa wonder why they'd even had a little girl. And now this.

"I think I'd better talk to your parents."

"C'mon," she said grabbing Jack's hand and tugging him toward the car. "You know you won't do that. You can't."

"Then promise me you won't make friends with strangers."

"Everybody's a stranger before you know them," she argued. "If you couldn't make friends with strangers, you'd be really lonely."

"You know what I mean," he warned.

"It was only you," she defended as they both got into the car.

The driver looked over his shoulder, glancing between the odd couple in back and the order sheet on the clipboard in his lap. "This says we stop at a rehab center at Forty-Seventh and Second, then we go to Long Island. Is that right?"

"Nope," said Jack. "Long Island first. Then, on the way back, I get out at Forty-Seventh."

Now that was a change in plans. "You're going with me?"

He nodded. "I'm seeing you safely inside."

Taking a deep breath, Melissa rolled her eyes. This was what she'd heard her mother call déjà vu. Hadn't she just had this exact same conversation with Jimmy Delaney? "The driver of the limousine is not going to drive away with me."

"Long Island first," said Jack.

As Melissa rattled off the street address she'd found on the invitation, the driver merely nodded, his expression blank. If it seemed strange to see a young African-American girl in a long, party dress giving a white man a ride to an alcohol rehabilitation center in a limo, he wasn't letting on. It wasn't the first time Melissa counted her lucky stars for having been born in New York. She had a sneaking suspicion her personal lifestyle would be cramped in other states she'd heard of, such as Wisconsin or Iowa. Of course, in Wisconsin, she *could* keep her horse in the front yard….

"Well," said Melissa suddenly, addressing Jack. "If you're going to Long Island, you might as well come to the party."

Finally, something made him laugh, and she was glad. Jack was starting to get a little serious for Melissa's taste. "Me? At Julia Darden's party? Now, how would we explain that?"

"I'll think of something," Melissa assured promptly.

Jack released a soft whistle. "Somehow, honey," he said, "I have absolutely no doubt you will."

Her spirits lifted. She smiled, glancing through the window at the white lights sparkling in the dark night, and she said, "Thank you. I'll take that as a compliment, Jack."

WATCHING THE SCENE BEFORE HER, Edie could almost forget her confused feelings about the man at her side. Almost. But Jimmy Delaney was pressed flush against her, since everyone was crowded into the service hallway between the ballroom and kitchen. His body felt better than she wanted to admit, too. Big, hard and hot. So, she concentrated her attention through the door, which was open, just a crack, so they could hear the speeches. Through the window in the door, Edie could survey her handiwork for the first time that night.

"If this doesn't prove the wedding curse on the Bennings is over," said Edie's Granny Ginny in a hushed tone, "I don't know what could."

"It's amazing," her mother whispered, finding Edie's hand in the mash of warm bodies and squeezing hard.

And it was. Since the ballroom was large for the rehearsal party, Paulie had built a floral partition, to give the illusion of a smaller space, but one that would allow for more guests once Sparky finished speaking. Earlier, Paulie had gotten confused about its placement, but it had been finished in ample time, and the flowers he'd brought for the tables were so beautiful Edie still didn't quite believe they were real. Everything looked even more impressive than it had in Edie's imagination.

Emma Goldstein from *Celebrity Weddings* magazine was managing the photographers and a videographer. All were getting close without being invasive, taking enough pictures to ensure Julia and Lorenzo would have wonderful memories forever. At the last minute, Edie had been so afraid that the white tablecloths and white, lavender-rimmed china would look uninspired, but crème underskirts graced the tables, falling beneath in gradations of white, and the lavender chargers were an interesting touch. In the end, everything looked exactly as Edie had intended—timeless and classic.

So far, the food had been a success, too. The fish had arrived, and people had raved about the salmon and duck entrées, as well as her father's presentations, which had included sprays of herbs and crisp, brightly colored vegetables. During a last-minute attack of nerves, Edie had worried that the long-stemmed, surreal lilies on the tables would obscure guests' views of each other, but that, too, had turned out to be untrue.

Julia's gown was nearly as gorgeous as Edie's dream confection, which she'd wear down the aisle tomorrow. Nearly ankle length, it was of a lavender crepe fabric that suited her, and it matched one of the desserts Edie's father was ready to wheel out, a two-foot-tall conical lavender cake covered with sugar rose petals.

"If my rehearsal dinner isn't at least this fabulous, I'll never forgive you," said Marley, her hushed voice coming from behind, as well as her hand that snaked briefly around Edie's waist. For a second, she felt her twin's body brush hers, and her throat got tight. It was hard to believe Edie's first niece or nephew was right behind her, growing in her sister's belly, and that just months away, she'd be holding that child. A sharp twinge came behind the pleasure, too, since Edie wanted her own, and she had to fight the urge to look at Jimmy. Even now, she could barely call him that. To her, he'd always be Seth. Only now did she really admit how much she'd been fantasizing about a future, one that would have included babies.

Damn. Why had she told him to come? What good would it do? He'd lied to her. And she could never keep seeing a man she didn't trust.

"Looks like they cleaned their plates," said her dad, drawing her from the unwanted thoughts.

"Wait until they see the desserts," Edie returned, feeling glad they'd added another. Once more, she felt an urge to glance at Jimmy. He looked really handsome in the suit he'd chosen. More like a best man or groom than her assistant.

"I just wish Sparky would finish his speech," put in Bridget. Because of a staff crunch, she'd wound up trading in one of her usually wild outfits for a white dress and matching apron that was trimmed in lavender, which Edie had chosen for the female wait staff.

"He is," whispered Edie.

"People are arriving for dessert," her sister whispered back. "I checked with Pete. A valet's parking cars, and people are milling in the foyer."

They had that covered. Everybody was being served drinks.

"All right," Sparky Darden was saying, speaking into a microphone that would soon be used by the lead singer of the band, and running a hand over a head left nearly bald by his chemotherapy. "I know this is where we wind things up for tonight." Pausing he chuckled. "Tomorrow, you'll be hearing more of me at the reception, I'm sure…."

As Edie listened to his continuing patter, she couldn't help but smile. No man had ever looked so proud. And it wasn't hard to believe he'd built a huge, thriving multimillion-dollar hotel empire all by his lonesome, either. He was a small, spry man, shorter than his gorgeous leggy daughter; his wife had been a Hollywood actress, and Julia had apparently gotten her mother's statuesque genes.

Despite that, and his long-term illness, Sparky Darden was one of those men who emanated raw, can-do energy. Call it drive or ambition, but the proverbial life force clearly emanated from deep within him. Everyone who'd ever met him had sensed he was special, destined to lead more than an average man's life. Julia had been a late baby for him, and now, at sixty-seven, he looked dapper, outfitted in a gray suit, which he wore with a lavender tie. Already, he'd spoken of his wife— of how he'd sensed her presence near him today, and of how, although she couldn't be here to see her only daughter marry, she was here in spirit.

"Yeah, I know I'm supposed to wrap it up," he was saying, "and end by announcing I'm not losing a daughter, but gaining a son. But I can't do that without acknowledging that the announcement of this wedding brought my biological son back to me, as well."

Most people present would know that story, one Edie and her family also knew intimately. "Years ago, before I met Julia's mother," Sparky explained, "I dated a woman in New Orleans, and while I didn't know it at the time, we had a son together, named Cash Champagne. As so many of you have heard, he found out about his half sister, Julia's, wedding, and arrived here in town, slipping into the life of a woman named Edie Benning, but then he met her sister Marley and now they're engaged."

Pausing, he smiled. "I've heard that's not all. Marley and Cash are going to have a baby. Which means this wedding brought me a grandchild. As Cash got to know Marley, I guess it must have softened his heart toward his old man—by that, I mean me—who was fool enough to abandon him and his mother while I was busy building my career. Yeah, he must have forgiven me, because he came by the house to meet me, and we've gotten to know each other, which means this wedding didn't just bring me a son, but it brought Julia a half brother she'd wanted to meet for years, and like I said, there's a baby on the way."

Grinning broadly, Julia quickly lifted a fork and tapped the side of her champagne glass, gamely shouting, "Hear, hear!" Then she nestled back into Lorenzo's arms and craned her head, looking toward the kitchen. Taking his cue, Cash thrust a hand through the crack in the door and waved. He'd opted to stay with Marley, helping the Bennings in the kitchen, although he would have been welcome to be a participant at the dinner.

"And there's more," continued Sparky, sending a huge smile in their direction. "Years ago, I started out doing the lowest level jobs in hotels I didn't have a dream of ever owning. Or at least, that's what I thought back then. But I did have the extreme pleasure of working with a dishwasher who had his own dreams of working on the other side of the kitchen with the chefs. And that man's name was Joe Benning."

Sparky lifted the microphone from the stand, and shifting his weight, he lowered his head and shook it, as if he simply couldn't believe how much time had passed. When he looked upward again, there were tears in his eyes. "Now, many more years passed," he said, speaking like a consummate storyteller. "And one night, while I was up late, wondering what the heck I'd been doing with my life, the way a man does when he gets sick, I thought of all the people I'd known who I'd never kept in touch with. Or who I felt I could have done favors for once my business really started to flourish...."

"And whaddya know?" Tilting back his head, Sparky laughed. "Right there, on an infomerical on TV, was a young woman named Edie Benning, advertising her new wedding-planning business in Manhattan. Since she had his same twinkling eyes, it didn't take long for me to figure out this Edie Benning was related to the same Joe Benning I used to know. And—" He flashed a giant grin, adding in an aside, "You were wondering when I'd circle back to talking about my own daughter's wedding, weren't you?"

Everyone laughed now. More listeners tapped the sides of their glasses in approval, and Edie's heart swelled. Despite all that had happened today, and that she was experiencing deeply ambivalent emotions about the man beside her, she couldn't believe Sparky was actually acknowledging her and her family. Planning the wedding really had been hard work. Six long months of it. And all under the gun, since there was so little time, and so many security risks. Pete had really done a great job, too. A couple of the security men in the room were carrying cameras, as if they were photographers. Others were outside. Most were out of sight.

As she had countless times, Edie silently damned whoever had sent the woman threatening letters. What could motivate a person to ruin another's joy? Well, whoever he was, he hadn't gotten away with it. Tomorrow, nearly a thousand people would be milling between this ballroom and the lawn outside. As soon as the rehearsal party was over, Edie and her father would be supervising the breakdown of the room.

"And," Sparky said, still talking, "since I just so happened to have a daughter who was getting married, and since Joe's daughter, Edie, just happened to have a wedding-planning business…"

During his long pause, laughter rippled through the room.

"Uh…could all of you behind the curtain do us a favor and step into the room for just a minute? Show us who's creating all the magic!"

Edie shook her head in protest, but so many people were crowded near the doorway that she had little choice but to file out with the others. Vaguely, she realized that Marley and Bridget were on either side of her, and that her parents were on the other side of Marley. Cash and Jimmy Delaney had hung back, receding further into the hallway, as had her grandmother.

"I give you the Bennings," announced Sparky. "My old friend Joe from so many years ago, who left his job as a dishwasher to follow his heart, not to mention his stomach. He's spent hours contemplating every morsel you've eaten." Just as Edis,e' father took a bow, Sparky continued, "And next is his wife, Viv, who's designed and made the gowns covering my daughter's gorgeous bod." A comment that made Julia squeal with glee, and another series of bright camera flashes wink from the four corners of the room, where photographers were positioned. Silently, musicians entered by a doorway opposite that to the kitchen, getting ready to file in behind Sparky and start playing.

"A bod that's been kept well honed by fitness trainer Marley Benning," Sparky continued. "And it was Bridget who designed the rings...."

As her sister curtsied gamely, Edie simply couldn't believe any of this was happening. It was so perfect. More than anything, she'd wanted this particular wedding to be a family event. She loved her family more than life, she thought now, and she'd been so afraid, as she and her sisters left home, that they'd grow apart...that nothing would emerge to help them maintain their ties and bind them together in the years of their adult lives.

But now...maybe this wedding wouldn't be the last they'd contribute to together. And Jimmy Delaney? Hadn't this wedding brought him to her, also? A man she'd been so sure was The One. A man who'd turned out to be a liar, but who'd followed her here, clearly wanting to be forgiven. Sparky hadn't mentioned it, but Bridget had found the love of her life through this wedding, also, since one of the rings she'd designed had turned out to be related to the Benning wedding curse. A curse Edie's grandmother was convinced had been lifted.

Had it? Edie glanced toward the kitchen, wondering if she could give Jimmy Delaney the absolution he sought. But she wasn't sure. What would have to happen for her to trust him again? She was so lost in thought that she barely heard her name.

"And last but not least," said Sparky Darden. "I give you Edie Benning. Wedding planner extraordinaire!"

As people turned and applauded, tears stung her eyes. Don't cry, she coached herself. But it was so hard. She'd dreamed of this wedding for so many years. So many of the components had been things she'd dreamed of when she was a kid, planning her own make-believe, fairy-tale wedding. And she'd followed her heart. All these years, she'd hung on to her personal vision. Sometimes, she wondered if anyone really knew how hard it had been, how many times she'd felt she'd taken a wrong turn, only to come back to her vision and follow her dream to open Big Apple Brides.

"Thank you," she managed to mouth when the applause died down, and then somehow, feeling as if she were floating on air, she turned and headed for the kitchen once more, only to be confronted with Jimmy.

"We figured it would all work out nicely," Sparky continued. "I gained a biological son. And—" he nodded toward Lorenzo "—another son of my heart. About Julia? Well, everybody knows that I've been smitten by my only baby since the day she was born. It goes without saying that anyone she loves, I love. So, no, I'll never lose a daughter." Replacing the microphone, he finished. "Because I could never let her go."

"Oh, Daddy!" Julia cried, rising from her chair and smacking Lorenzo soundly on the lips before rushing toward her father. "You're so sweet, Daddy!"

Sensing the moment had arrived, the musicians swarmed into the bandstand area and began taking up instruments. A second later, a waltz was playing, and Julia was dancing with her father. They turned in slow circles, their eyes locked, their lips stretched into smiles. Edie was too far away to see, but she'd bet both had tears in their eyes. Right on cue, as the wait staff surreptitiously removed plates and began rolling in desserts for the buffet, Pete began leading in the guests who'd been in the foyer. Everything was so perfectly choreographed that Edie was totally overwhelmed.

"Oh, look," Edie found herself whispering breathlessly, as Sparky guided Julia in the direction of her and Lorenzo's table, then stopped beside his son-in-law, who stood. The two men hugged, and then Sparky gave Lorenzo Julia's hand. The moment couldn't have been more perfect.

"You did it," said a voice beside her.

It was Jimmy Delaney's. And there was no denying how her heart swelled. Damn her for caring, but she'd wanted to impress him. Turning her head, she caught his eyes. The second they locked, the old feeling was there—the sudden infusion of heat, the sense of inexplicable connectedness. Somehow, she knew she could forgo seeing this man for the next ten years, and if they met again, it would be exactly like this. A stream of energy coursing between them, unstoppable and eternal. Unless they were together, whatever was between them would feel like unfinished business.

"Thanks," she managed, turning to head into the kitchen again.

But Jimmy wouldn't let things go at that. His hand found her cheek, the fingers trailing down her skin, his eyes holding hers as surely as a vise. "You really pulled it off, Edie," he said simply.

She'd never felt so transparent. She felt as if he'd seen straight through her, into her soul, into her deepest, most cherished dreams and desires, and because of that, she couldn't fight the lump that formed in her throat. "Thanks," she said again. But this time, she meant it.

Then something darting in the periphery of her vision captured her attention. At first she thought it was a flash from the cameras of one of the *Celebrity Weddings* photographers, but then she realized it was a little girl. "Who's that?" she asked, not really expecting an answer.

She pointed to a girl in a long white dress, just in time to see her ducking under the cloth of a serving table. It wasn't the flower girl, or the ring bearer, and they were supposed to be the only two children here. Both were related to Lorenzo Santini. "Who's that?" Edie asked. And then, without waiting for a response, "What's she doing?"

"I don't know," said Jimmy with a frown. "But whatever it is, I can guarantee she's up to no good."

"You know her?"

"She's one of my students."

"One of your students?" Edie echoed.

"Arrested for shoplifting and credit card debt."

"But why would she be here? What's her name?"

"Melissa Jones."

Relief gushed through Edie's system. Nothing untoward had happened. Everything was fine. "Her parents are here," she explained. "Julia must have forgotten to inform me about a change in the guest list. Melissa's dad's an ex NFL guy, now a sportscaster for the networks, and so Lorenzo knows him. Because he follows all the games, he knows the guys on the team, too, and I guess it's political. Media coverage brings a higher profile to all of them—"

When she nodded, Jimmy followed her gaze to where a number of oversize men were grouped together near a drink table. They were a buoyant bunch, jostling and punching each other. The man who was Melissa's dad was in the mix. "I remember him," Jimmy suddenly said. He didn't follow sports, but his father did. "Steelers."

Edie nodded. "That's him. Tyrone Jones."

"The team looks pretty competitive," he said.

Given how they'd been interacting over the past few hours, the segue to more ordinary conversation felt forced. "Yeah," Edie managed, keeping her tone level, even though it felt like a charade, since her heart was breaking. "They are. Rumor has it, there are going to be a lot of trades on the team. Guys are going to be bumped. It wasn't their greatest season." She turned away. "Look, I'd better get back...."

Another camera flash caught her attention and she glanced in that direction, only to have her lips part in surprise. Melissa Jones had drawn back the tablecloth under the dessert table and was snapping pictures of Julia Darden, without a flash. She couldn't help but chuckle. "How cute. She must be taking pictures for your class. She'd better hope Emma Goldstein and the guys from *Celebrity Weddings* don't realize they've got professional competition."

When she glanced at Jimmy, he was shaking his head in disgust. "Why that devious little..." he began.

And then he started toward the little girl, his long legs moving him quickly across the ballroom.

11

As HE CROSSED THE ROOM, his dark shoes clicking on the black-and-white tile floor, Jimmy uttered a soft expletive under his breath, then he almost stopped in his tracks, realizing he was about to take his anger about the situation with Edie out on an eleven-year-old, when it was really no one's fault but his own. Or was he? After all, Edie had said Melissa hadn't been on the guest list, and yet she was here, taking pictures. Why? She'd known he was aware of the party, so she could have mentioned her own invitation when they were on the church steps. "Wait a minute," he muttered. Had she been trying to get information about the party from him?

Maybe. Because she looked guilty as hell. Seeing him coming, Melissa ducked under the serving table again, pulling the white cloth in front of her like a curtain. "As if that's going to work," he said, shaking his head.

He could sense Edie catching up, her strides matching his, and nothing more than that made his heart ache. She moved so perfectly with him, he couldn't help but be reminded of how it felt when they were making love. Couldn't she feel how right they were together? That they'd never be happy without each other, not after the taste of what they'd shared? For a second, he wished they were alone again, back on the church steps, or in

Big Apple Brides, and that he could put his arms around her, pull her into an embrace and beg her to forget what a horse's behind he'd been.

"She's your student?" she echoed.

"Yeah," he said simply.

Whole worlds seemed to pass between them in all that had remained unsaid. Silently, he cursed Fate for having him find her at a time in his life when he was so unprepared. An image of the guys at the Suds Bar flitted into his mind when he shot her another glance, and for the umpteenth time, he really wished he could take back the past couple years of his life. Had he really spent his evenings drinking imported beers and shooting darts with guys who made the Marx Brothers look sane? Had he really been doing so when he could have been building a career and raising a family, the way Ches had?

Concern played on Edie's features, and he didn't blame her. Now that he'd seen the party she'd planned come alive, he was even more impressed by how much time, energy and emotion she'd put into this. She was brilliant. More than a woman who could carry her own weight in a partnership. Edie Benning was a visionary.

Her voice hitched with worry. "What are you going to do?"

"Just ask a few questions," he said as they reached the table.

Leaning, he lifted the edge of the tablecloth and glanced beneath just in time to see Melissa scramble backward, scooting on her behind, one hand wrapped protectively over the camera in her hand, the other gripping the handle of an oversize white pocketbook. Quickly, he crouched, and just as she scrambled further backward, he gasped, seeing that her heel had caught an edge of the cloth. "Don't," he said in sudden warning, seeing she was pulling it with her as she moved, but she only scurried farther back.

"Oh, no," cried Edie sharply, just as everything started to slide toward the table's edge.

"Damn," he muttered, swiping the cloth a second too late, then hanging on to it as he circled the table. Unfortunately, it didn't stop the rows of neatly aligned dessert forks, napkins, tiered trays of petits fours and stack of china plates from spilling over the side, carried on the wave of the moving cloth.

A loud crash sounded, then the tinkling of shattering shards of china on the tiles. Everything seemed to happen all at once. Loud footsteps sounded. Cameras flashed. Behind Jimmy, musicians continued to play, but missed notes. As dancing feet paused and people murmured, Melissa scrambled to her feet, further scattering bits of china and looking so stricken that Jimmy's heart actually softened. Obviously, she'd been trying hard to look ladylike, but the dress wasn't her style, which ran to jeans and sneakers. Her sash was undone, the leggings were bagging at the knees and the bobby pins skewering her hair were lopsided. Her mouth was stretched wide, the teeth gritted, and her unblinking eyes were as round as saucers.

Edie looked just as upset. Quickly turning, he placed a hand on her arm and gave a quick squeeze. "It'll be all right. Don't worry."

Edie nodded.

But they both knew it wouldn't. Pete Shriver was striding across the room and Bridget and Marley appeared, rushing toward the scene with a bag. Kneeling, they began picking up broken china. Viv and Joe had raced behind, carrying another stack of plates and fresh silverware. Glancing down, Jimmy realized he'd stepped in the petits fours. Grabbing a napkin, he tried to clean his sole, just as footsteps pounded closer.

A woman's voice said, "Melissa?"

When he turned, he saw Melissa's parents coming toward them at breakneck speed. The wife—Jimmy didn't know her name—was moving faster than her husband, Tyrone. Both were good-looking people, the kind you'd stare at in a crowd, and they were dressed to the nines—him, in the glamorous steel-colored suit he'd noticed earlier and that probably, given his size, had to be tailor-made. She was wearing a diaphanous silver cocktail dress with spaghetti straps and a stylishly uneven, ruffled hem.

"What are you doing here, Melissa?" she demanded.

Just as the woman dropped to her knees, Melissa lunged, flying into her mother's arms, the camera and pocketbook banging against her side. "And that's my pocketbook! How did you get here?"

So they didn't know their daughter had come, Jimmy thought. Before he could ask any questions, Melissa crooned, "I just wanted to be with you and Daddy. Oh, Mommy, I missed you so much. Mrs. Rodriguez fell asleep, so I just put on the beautiful party dress you were so nice to buy for me, for Easter. I found the invitation and came to be with you. I missed you so much after you left, and Julia Darden looks so nice. I've seen her picture in the papers, so I didn't think she'd mind if there was another guest at her party."

Pausing, Melissa giggled mischievously. "And it's not like I take up a lot of space, since I'm just a kid."

Jimmy was stunned. He'd never have believed a kid could lay it on so thick. He almost wanted to laugh. Glancing at Edie, he rolled his eyes. She shrugged. Not that she looked as if she'd forgive him. The second their eyes met was brief—just a heartbeat. But maybe he'd never hated himself more. In the depths of her blue eyes now was something guarded, a look of mistrust that hadn't been present before. And he was the man who'd put it there.

Tyrone's voice claimed his attention. "Answer your mother. How did you get here, Melissa?"

"I brought her," someone interjected.

Everyone turned toward the voice in surprise, and Jimmy could barely mask his confusion. It was the homeless guy he'd seen in the pictures Melissa had brought to class. Given the photographs she'd taken of the man, it was clear he'd undergone a rapid change in the past few weeks, one that was evident in more than his close shave, haircut and freshly pressed shirt and jeans. Jimmy couldn't help but notice that he seemed transformed. Despite the situation, there was a lively, determined intensity in his sharp blue eyes.

Melissa's father looked fit to kill. "And you are?"

"The name's Jack Stevens," the man said.

"Jack Stevens!" This time, the speaker was Julia Darden, who'd dragged Lorenzo over to see what was happening, and Jimmy felt his heart sinking. Damn. He'd hoped to get everybody moving away from the center of the room, but now...had the guy really said he was Jack Stevens?

"The photographer?" he asked.

"It's a long story."

"You were dressing as a homeless man," Jimmy said, the truth hitting him.

"Huh?" Jack stared at him as if he was crazy. "Uh…no. What are you talking about? I'm really a homeless guy. Why would I pretend to be living on the streets, and—"

"To get your pictures," Jimmy interjected, just the way he and his buddies had. "To get close to the subjects." Not that it explained how close he'd gotten in Lorenzo's locker room.

Julia shrieked, "Pete? Where's Pete Shriver? Will someone get Pete?"

"I'm right here," said Pete. "Right behind you. I'm listening."

Cameras were flashing. "Great," Jimmy muttered. "Just great. Look—" He shot Pete a pointed glance. "Can we take this somewhere else?"

"Yeah, folks. He's right. There's a party out here. Why don't we all head for the kitchen."

"I can explain everything," Jack was saying as he began moving in that direction. "And I really think I should. I mean, I really don't feel comfortable with any of this, and I'm worried about Melissa—"

Tyrone still looked livid. "Who are you?" he said, shooting off questions, rapid-fire. "Where did you come from? And how do you know our daughter?"

"Well," Jack began. "It's a long story." As they all moved quickly toward the kitchen, in a growing mass of people, each was trying to jockey closer to the center of the action, to hear what was going on. Julia and Lorenzo edged out the Bennings and Jones families, followed by Pete Shriver, as Jack Stevens lunged into an account of his life reversals. Despite himself, Jimmy couldn't help but feel some sympathy, especially when he talked about his misfortunes with the health care system, since Jimmy had experienced some of his own. When he saw Jack Stevens's eyes actually growing misty, Jimmy realized that, whatever the man had done, he truly hadn't meant to harm anyone.

"Reversals happen when you least expect them," he was saying. "They come when you're unprepared."

"A homeless man," Jimmy muttered under his breath, wondering how Melissa had met him. And if she'd been letting the man use her camera. No wonder his buddies from the Suds Bar had never heard of the guy.

"And so you took pictures of Lorenzo?" Julia suddenly cut in. She was moving right behind Jack, her long, slender-fingered hands gripped tightly around the delicate lavender dress, hiking it well above her calves, so she could move with more dexterity. She looked just as mad as Melissa's mother and Edie.

"Not exactly," ventured Jack as they neared the door to the service hallway. "It was really Melissa—"

"That's Jimmy Delaney!" Melissa nearly shouted.

Jimmy felt his heart drop to his feet. Unbelievable. How could an eleven-year-old cause so much commotion and damage? He watched in stunned stupefaction as Julia forgot all about Jack and whirled in his direction, just as Melissa had intended. "What?" She gaped at him, then glanced at Edie. "You're Seth Bishop."

Of course, since he'd been introduced as Seth Bishop, not only to the Dardens, but also to Edie's family, he and Edie hadn't been about to explain the truth tonight, when they'd reached the estate. Out of the corner of his eye, he could see the surprised expressions on the Bennings' faces. That, he decided, was even worse than Julia's fury. About Edie's expression, he simply didn't know. He didn't have the nerve to look.

"It's a long story," said Edie with a sigh. "But it really is Jimmy Delaney. He told me his name was Seth Bishop."

Great. He'd been reduced to an "it." As in "it" is Jimmy Delaney. Not "he."

"He has an order of protection," Melissa rushed on, obviously hoping to steer the conversation away from her own wrongdoing. "He's not supposed to take pictures of Julia, right? I know because I'm in his photography class on Saturdays, for wayward kids."

Tyrone gasped. "Jimmy Delaney is teaching your class?"

Apparently, Tyrone knew his name, probably from pictures he'd taken of ballplayers for the tabloids. But it wasn't exactly Jimmy's fault that such men got themselves into so much trouble with women and drugs. He'd about had it. Hell, he'd seen the lonely look in Melissa's eyes. "If you kept up with your daughter," he couldn't help but say, "you'd have known who was teaching her class."

"It's not *our* fault," Tyrone defended. "The court system set that up! We had no choice!"

"Placing blame isn't the issue, Tyrone," his wife insisted, trying to keep the peace.

"Judge Diana Little may have sent Melissa to my class," Jimmy muttered, shooting a glance toward Edie, then wishing he hadn't. She was pressing two fingers to the bridge of her nose as if she was getting the world's worst migraine headache. He knew how it felt, too. They were both head, not stomach, people. It was one of the many things they had in common.

Maybe it was sheer perversity that made him plunge on, or maybe the fact that he couldn't afford to be blamed for anything more than he'd really done. He wanted back in Edie's good graces. "It's not exactly my fault Melissa maxed out the credit cards and got caught shoplifting in Bloomingdale's."

Tyrone looked as if a lightbulb had just gone off inside his head. "The locker room," he muttered, turning toward his daughter. "You got those pictures of Lorenzo. It wasn't this man, Jack Stevens, was it? We were driving ourselves crazy at work, trying to figure out how the guy got into our studio, past all the security guards." Pivoting, he gaped at Jimmy. "I can't believe this. Did you put my daughter—an eleven-year-old kid—up to taking pictures for you?"

Now this was a new twist. When Jimmy glanced at Edie, bands seemed to circle around his chest, squeezing so tightly that he couldn't breathe. Dammit, didn't this foolish man know what he was doing to Jimmy's love life? "This is all wrong," he begged Edie, no longer caring that anyone else was even there. "I didn't put Melissa up to this."

Color had drained from Edie's face, leaving it chalk-white, and strangely, she'd never looked more beautiful, her wide eyes almost the exact blue of the dress, under the soft lights in the room. She looked appalled, as if she'd known he was a jerk, but that he'd now sunk to unfathomable depths. "How could you?"

He blew out a sigh of frustration. "I didn't." Moving closer, he implored her with his eyes. "Everything I've said all day is true, Edie. I want you. I love you. I want to marry you. Do you hear me? I came to work for you so that I could get into this wedding, and I admitted that to you, but you changed me, just like I said. You've got to listen."

"You're not Seth Bishop?" asked Julia, as if still unable to believe her ears. "You're really Jimmy Delaney?"

He stared at the woman he'd shot pictures of so many times, and always against her will. Up close, she was even more of a knockout than through a zoom lens. Taller than he, she was willowy in the way models were, the skin of her face as smooth as a baby's, her features, even when angry, classic and even. The only difference was how smart she looked. Up close, Julia Darden's eyes sparked with an intelligence he'd never noticed before now, not even when he'd first met her.

"Look," he said, meaning it. "I'm sorry. I've told Edie how I got started taking celebrity photographs. My mother was sick and I needed the money. That's the truth…uh, Ms. Darden. But after she got well, I kept on working in that industry. I really am sorry. I didn't mean to hurt anyone. That was never my intention."

Julia considered. "You took a job working for Edie because you wanted to sneak some shots of me?"

"Yes."

"But then you didn't, because you fell in love with her?"

He turned toward Edie, whose face was immobile. "Yes," he said once more. Unsure which woman he was addressing now, he added, "Please, you've got to believe—"

Before he could finish, a fist appeared from nowhere; his attention had been so fixed on Edie that Jimmy didn't see it until it was too late. In the instant before knuckles crashed against his temple, splitting flesh, Jimmy realized the attacker was Sparky Darden. Then he heard Julia shriek and say, "Oh, no, another one of those letters is in Lorenzo's pocket!"

And then everything went black.

STOP THE WEDDING *tomorrow or the bride will die.*

Pinching the bridge of her nose between a forefinger

and thumb and wishing her head would stop pounding, Edie stared down at the note, which was in a plastic bag on the kitchen table. The letters had been cut from a magazine, and Pete Shriver, who was pacing around the room had schooled everybody not to touch it.

Pete's men were locking down the whole place, questioning all the guests at the estate, since one of them had presumably put the letter into Lorenzo's pocket. According to Lorenzo, the letter hadn't been in his pocket when he'd entered the party. All of which meant that, for all practical purposes, the rehearsal dinner was over.

Right now, Pete's men were also confiscating all the cameras, including Melissa's, and in turn, that meant that Emma Goldstein and the others from *Celebrity Weddings* were none too happy. If Edie had created a story version of the worst-case scenario for this evening, this would be it. Even now, her mind was reeling, trying to deny it was happening.

But it was. Melissa Jones, who'd been sentenced to be in Jimmy's class had gotten the idea, after meeting him, to take pictures of celebrities by using her dad's position at the network. In turn, she'd coerced Jack Stevens to be her middleman at the tabloids, and he agreed, since he was really at rock bottom and willing to try anything, even something questionable, to right his situation. Just as all that was coming to the fore, only moments ago, Melissa had exposed Jimmy, so Sparky had decked him, and then Julia had discovered another poison-pen letter of the sort she'd been getting since October. Had Edie really thought the wedding would occur without Julia and Lorenzo getting any more hate mail?

"I can't take this," Julia said, her voice strained as she leaned against the kitchen door. "I really can't. And to think it wasn't a stranger! That one of our guests has probably been threatening me all along! And this time, they actually put the letter in Lorenzo's pocket." Crossing her arms over the waist of the lavender dress, she shook her head, as if trying to process the betrayal. "Oh, Lozo," she added, using his pet name. "They could have hurt you."

"Or you," her fiancé said grimly.

Edie knew how Julia felt. Not that her life had been threatened. But the man with whom she'd been sharing a bed had actually entered her life using a false name. She could certainly relate to the sense of violation. What was wrong with people? she fumed, her mind suddenly filling with other stories of betrayal from news headlines. She'd even seen a woman on *Dr. Phil* who'd corresponded with a man for years on the Internet, pledging her undying devotion, only to find out he was years older than he'd claimed, and married with kids.

"I'm so sorry, baby," crooned Lorenzo now, pulling Julia into his arms and sprinkling kisses over her face and hair.

"Who would do this?" she asked rhetorically. "And the night before our wedding?"

"I don't know," continued Lorenzo, "but Pete will catch him. I'm sure of it. And I love you, right? And you love me. That's the important thing, huh?"

"Yeah. So, I think we should…" Her voice trailed off. *Call off the wedding.*

That's what she was going to say. Edie's mind whirled. Not now, she thought. Not when we're so close. The ceremony was less than twenty-four hours away. The plans were so perfect… The dress, music, flowers, reception. Edie would sooner die than see it all go to waste. But it could. The Dardens were wealthy enough that they could walk away, even after having spent so much. Especially if Julia's life was in danger. And if she was honest, Edie could understand. Under these circumstances, her father wouldn't let her get married.

Somehow, she managed to seat herself at one of the stools surrounding the table, unable to believe the crew that had assembled. As much as she was trying to ignore him, Jimmy Delaney had chosen a seat next to her, close enough that she could smell cologne mixing with the clean scent of his skin, a scent she'd found maddening in bed and which she now cursed for teasing memories to the surface of her awareness. Definitely, this was the wrong time to replay nights they'd lain in her bed together, staring out the window and wishing on stars.

God, her head was throbbing. In a few moments, she was sure she'd start feeling white-hot needles of pain behind her eyes. Even worse, it was Jimmy who noticed. He got up, then a moment later, a large hand that had caressed each inch of her until her mind was lost to blissful distraction appeared again from behind. Soundlessly, he set down two tablets and a glass of water. His body appeared next, folding into a chair, on the side of her opposite Jack Stevens.

Not that Jimmy was in much better shape than she. Sparky Darden was approaching seventy, but he worked out daily with a professional trainer, and Jimmy had been caught completely off guard. Now his eye was showing signs of turning bright purple, and he was pressing a slab of dinner meat against the bruise at her father's insistence.

Traitor, she couldn't help but think. Her parents were supposed to hate Jimmy Delaney every bit as much as she did right now. But her father and Cash had jumped into the fray, pulling Jimmy from the floor while Pete held Sparky Darden at bay, then they'd hauled Jimmy into the kitchen. From the opposite side of the room, Sparky was still sizing him up, looking as if he'd like to punch him once more, for causing his daughter so much grief. Violating eleven orders of protection hadn't exactly endeared Jimmy to the father of the bride. But everyone else seemed to have been snowed by his story. Did they believe he'd had a change of heart? That he really loved her?

She glanced away from him. Melissa and her parents were seated at one end of the table. Edie's own family—Granny Ginny, her parents and her sisters, Bridget and Marley, as well as Cash Champagne—were seated at the other end. The man who'd been homeless and who Melissa Jones had conned into fencing pictures of Lorenzo, which she'd taken, was seated next to Edie, looking as if he'd rather be anywhere else in the world.

She didn't blame him. Whatever strange turns Jack Stevens's life had taken since he'd met the mischievous Melissa Jones, he didn't seem like a bad person, and he seemed sincerely concerned about Melissa's welfare. "I can't help but feel this is all my fault," he was saying. "When Melissa started bringing me food, I should have rung the bell and told you what was going on…."

Melissa was crying now, and despite her behavior, Edie couldn't help but feel sorry for her. She was trying to be quiet, but sobs were racking her shoulders, and above all, she seemed to feel remorseful about exposing Jimmy. "I'm sorry," she said in a small, broken voice. "Everything was supposed to be so super tonight, but

I messed it all up." She looked at her parents. "I wanted a horse. That's all. Just a stupid horse."

Her parents sent each other long looks over the tops of her head. Then her mother said, "Melissa, we just don't understand you. You have everything a little girl could want. We got you your dream canopy bed last year, remember? And all the new spring clothes?"

Anything her mother said only made her cry harder. "I just wanted to get one friend," she muttered. "Then I met Jack. And I was in Jimmy's class, too. And so, it was like I had two friends at the same time. It was so nice. Mrs. Rodriguez only watches TV. If I'm really good she might play one game of Old Maid, but that's all."

"Honey." Her mother crouched down lower, to look into her daughter's eyes. "I play Old Maid with you, don't I?"

Melissa shook her head so hard that a bobby pin sprang loose. "Nope," she claimed, her chin quivering, her eyes shimmering with tears. "Three weeks ago. On a Tuesday. For only fifteen minutes before Daddy called and said you had to go to a fund-raiser."

Tyrone appeared shocked. He, too, bent lower to get a better look at his daughter. "Do you want us to spend more time with you? Is that really the problem?"

"It's all for you," her mother said quickly. "Everything we do."

"No, it's not," Tyrone returned, his eyes meeting hers. "What Jimmy Delaney said is right. I hate to admit it. But that judge, Diane Little, intimated the same things. We're never home, Chynna. And it's…it's not working. We've got to make some changes. We're always on the go…always trying to be somebody. But it never stops, does it? The NFL wasn't enough. The network job. The parties. We're always saying that we're going to slow down in the future, spend more time at home...."

Melissa's tears had dried on her face, and she was glancing between her parents with a heartbreaking expression of hope. "That's exactly right," Jack Stevens put in. "Melissa's a good kid. She told me all about the shoplifting...."

As he plunged once more into his own past, Edie could only shake her head and thank her lucky stars for her family. Compared to all the other people around her, they were the most sane, stable, lovable and available people imaginable. Feeling something rub against her thigh, she glanced down—only to see Jimmy venture a touch, brushing his finger on her thigh. For a second, she watched as if mesmerized, as it glided along the powder-blue jersey knit dress. She'd bought it for comfort, since she'd anticipated being here all night breaking down the tables for the party, then setting up the chairs for tomorrow's wedding.

Oh, please, don't let Julia cancel, she suddenly thought.

But the other woman seemed to read her mind. Lifting on her tiptoes to kiss Lorenzo who, unlike all the other men in the room, was actually taller than her, Julia headed toward Edie, looking more like a floating goddess than a woman. As she sank almost to her haunches in front of Edie, what seemed like miles of lavender crepe swirled around her, and as she closed her impossibly long fingers over Edie's, Edie swallowed hard around the aching knot in her throat, knowing what was coming.

"Edie," Julia began. "I'm really sorry, but..."

That's when she lost it. Her swollen eyes were already burning, but now she felt tears pushing free. *Damn all of them! Everybody here!* she thought illogically.

She'd been on pins and needles for months. And worst of all, she loved Jimmy Delaney. Until the day she died, she was sure he'd be fixed in her mind with the name Seth Bishop, no matter what she did to convince herself of the truth. He'd been her dream man. Her fantasy. He'd brought her body to heights of awareness that she knew no other man ever would. And they were on the same wavelength. Connected in some inexplicable way that she didn't want to deny.

"I'm sorry, Edie," Julia said softly. "We got another one of those letters. I know someone's trying to terrorize us. And I know we shouldn't give in to that."

"You don't understand," Edie couldn't help but whisper. "It was my wedding, too."

Julia's dark eyes had filled with tears, also. This wasn't easy for her. Edie watched as they splashed down her cheeks, but Julia was smiling through them, too. "That's right," she said, her hands tightening on Edie's. "It's the most perfect wedding."

It was. But the fact only made a sob escape from between Edie's lips. Quickly, she pressed her fingers to her lips, to stop the sound. Surely, Julia wouldn't let all this go to waste. "I worked so hard. I...imagined every detail."

"You did," Julia agreed, her lips stretching into a tear-touched smile. "Because it's yours."

Suddenly, out of the corner of her eye, she saw the bulk of another body that edged Julia out of the way. And then, all at once, it was Jimmy, not Julia, who was kneeling in front of her. "Edie," he said simply. "Forgive me. Marry me."

Her mind was reeling. What was he thinking? Was Julia suggesting…?

Julia's voice cut in. "I'm too scared to go through with this. I want to get married. Now. Tonight." Julia turned toward her father and Lorenzo. "You both know I'd be happy with a civil service. I wanted to go to Vegas when Lozo proposed. And when he gave me…" Reaching for the chain around her neck, she drew the charm from her bodice, so it was visible—the pop can tab Lorenzo had slipped onto her finger long before the ring she now wore, which Bridget had designed. "This is my real ring. And I'll always wear it around my neck. I just want to be married. To know no one can stop us. There's got to be a judge who'll do this tonight. Daddy, I was going through with such a big wedding for you, but…"

"Your safety's more important," Sparky Darden said quickly.

"I…want one more wedding gift, Daddy."

"Anything, Julia. You know that."

"Uh…I think there should still be a wedding here tomorrow, even if it's not mine."

When Julia glanced between her father, Edie and Jimmy, Edie felt her whole world slide off-kilter. Surely, Edie was dreaming. Or she'd entered some crazy alternative universe. Was Julia Darden really offering her own dream wedding to Edie, who'd planned it? And to Jimmy, who'd been the bane of her existence? Jack Stevens had sure been telling the truth when he said that reversals in life happened quickly; they came in the wink of an eye, when you were least prepared, and before you even knew they'd occurred, your whole life had changed.

"Life happens in a heartbeat," she found herself whispering.

And because the man before her was on the exact same wavelength, he whispered back, "It turns on a dime, Edie."

One minute, she'd been standing in Big Apple Brides helping a couple named Stacy and Reggie, who had yet to return for their next consulting appointment. The next, Jimmy Delaney had appeared, staring at her through the windows of her shop, through a confection of hope chests, winged mannequins and champagne glasses.

Sparky Darden said, "By all means. This is the perfect solution."

"Will you marry me, Edie?" Jimmy asked.

From somewhere, she heard Granny Ginny sigh. "See? Didn't I tell everyone? I knew the Benning wedding curse was over."

But those old family myths seemed so far away now. Like ancient history. And suddenly, she guessed if Julia Darden could forgive Jimmy, she could, too. "Yes," she whispered, right before his lips brushed hers. "I guess we've got a lot of phone calls to make tonight," she managed to say to Jimmy as he drew away, wanting to pinch herself, since everything felt so incredibly unreal.

He said, "I only want my parents here."

"So do I," she whispered. She couldn't wait to meet them. Her mind was racing. Yes…she was going to have to cancel the Dardens' guests. That would take hours. The tables for the rehearsal dinner had to be taken down, and the setup for tomorrow put into place.

And then she'd have to call her own guests. For the first time in her life, she wished she had twenty sisters, instead of just two. But then, her sisters were truly the best. She glanced toward them, and both were standing by her parents. Absolutely everybody had tears in their eyes.

"Oh, dear," Viv Benning said simply.

Joe hooked his arm through his wife's and merely smiled.

"Go, sis," said Bridget.

Said Marley, "Well done."

12

EXACTLY THREE HOURS LATER, Saint John the Divine, which had been closed for the night, was reopened. That happened just moments after Tyrone and Chynna Jones called their best friend, the minister. Then the wedding party, still clad in finery from the rehearsal dinner, gathered before Judge Diana Little. When told the happy outcome of the events in which she'd played such a large hand, and in which two people she'd convicted had been transformed, the judge happily cut short her political dinner to officiate over Julia Darden and Lorenzo Santini's vows.

Seated in a pew, Edie felt Jimmy's hand close over hers, and she upturned her own, twining her fingers tightly with his. "It's really the same wedding," she whispered, biting back a smile.

"But with no publicity," Jimmy whispered back, "since it's not at the house. And so, there's no possibility of any harm coming to either of them."

She shook her head. "I wonder who could have been threatening her?"

"Who knows?"

"Well, this is the best of all possible worlds," she added as Julia, looking as resplendent in the lavender dress as Edie imagined she, herself, would the next day, in the dream gown she and her mother had designed together, turned toward Lorenzo and said, "I do."

Leaning closer, Jimmy whispered. "Not the best of all possible worlds. Not until tomorrow. When you marry me."

"Good point," Edie whispered.

"Do you, Jimmy Delaney, take Edie Benning to be your lawful wedded wife?"

As she heard the words, Edie still couldn't believe the fairy tale that had swept her off her feet in the past twenty-four hours. Or that twice in that time, she was facing Judge Diana Little, albeit this time as a bride. Or that she really was the first Benning to get married. After all, Marley and Bridget had managed to get engaged first. Or finally, that they'd really pulled off all the changes in plans. Her parents and Granny Ginny were seated right behind her, and Jimmy's folks had managed to pack and make it into town on the red-eye; there had even been time to spare for Jimmy's mother to find a new dress and get her hair done. Marley and Bridget were beside her, dressed in white. And Jimmy's best friend, Ches, had been able to stand as his best man. Melissa had agreed to be their flower girl.

According to Pete, Julia and Lorenzo were taking off for the trip they'd planned, and as far as Edie knew, they'd already gone. Suddenly, thoughts of her natural father, Jasper, flitted into Edie's mind, as well as of Marissa Jennings and Forrest Hartley, whose romance was at the heart of the wedding curse that Granny Ginny had once claimed affected her granddaughter's prospects. Edie smiled. Years ago, when she'd first dreamed of starting Big Apple Brides, she'd somehow hoped that the business would bring good Karma. And maybe it had. Surely, the wedding curse had ended now, if it had ever really existed….

Edie's eyes were fixed on Jimmy's, and suddenly, she almost wished she'd chosen to wear a veil, precisely for the reason she hadn't—she felt so, well…*bare*, as if her emotions were exposed for all the world to see. At least her eyes felt dry. Since last night, she'd felt sure she'd cried out all her tears.

At least until Jimmy said, "I do."

She felt them then, pushing once more at her eyelids. Everything suddenly felt positively overwhelming. For good and ill, you could turn a corner in life, and suddenly, everything changed. After six months of work, her lifelong dream vision had come completely alive before her very eyes. Chairs were arranged in neat rows behind her, in the Dardens' ballroom. Paulie had brought truckloads of the most exquisite white roses, and they banked sky-high, gleaming windows overlooking the tents on the lawn. The windows were so clean that Edie could barely even tell they were there, and the day beyond was perfect, with a cloudless cerulean sky. And, of course, she was standing with Jimmy beneath a garden arbor so sweetly scented that every breath made her feel as if she was about to topple from her high-heeled shoes, into a good, old-fashioned swoon.

Yes, suddenly, she felt positively faint. Judge Diana's voice seemed to come from a million miles away. "Do you, Edie, take Jimmy to be your lawful wedded husband…"

Her hands clutched, her twining fingers gripping the stems of the roses she carried. When the judge's voice stopped, she took a deep breath, the scent of the roses and Jimmy knifing to her lungs, and said, "I do. Oh, yes."

Somehow, she'd expected him to lean slowly and kiss her. Instead, he merely looked at her a long moment, his eyes dancing, looking as dark as the tuxedo he wore, one that Viv had been up half the night altering for him. His voice was as smooth as velvet. "You're sure?"

She nodded.

"Good. Because I need you to keep me in line," he said, his lips broadening into a grin.

As he angled his head lower, she whispered, "No more transgressions."

"I promise," he whispered back, and then suddenly, he leaned, hooked his arms behind her knees and lifted her into an embrace against his chest. Only then did he kiss her. It was a good thing she was in his arms, she thought vaguely, when she felt the blistering brush of heat, and salty warm tip of his tongue tracing her lips. Somewhere, far off, the guests were laughing in delight and applauding, and nearer, Bridget's fiancé, Dermott roused the assembled musicians to begin playing.

Turning, Jimmy ended the kiss, whirling her around, making the white fabric of her skirt fan out like rays of light. As he did, she followed the sudden impulse to throw the bouquet. Oh, she knew she was supposed to wait, but this way, tossing it just a foot away, she absolutely ensured that her twin, Marley, caught it.

"Thanks, sis," Marley said, smiling, catching it by the petals, her hand returning, as it had so often lately, to her belly, as if protecting the unborn child inside.

Edie would have responded, but already, Jimmy was charging down the long white runner, as if he had no intention of even staying for the reception. As if he couldn't get out of here fast enough. When they reached the end, they were in for a final surprise, because a camera suddenly flashed. Another quick flash came right

behind it, and then in shock, both Edie and Jimmy simultaneously realized that Julia Darden, who apparently hadn't yet left for her honeymoon, had defied
security, to take their wedding pictures, and that another photographer was snapping pictures of her doing
so.

"Reversals," Edie whispered with new tears in her
eyes.

"There's one thing I'm never going back on," he
whispered, his lips catching hers once more as he
headed for a door, leading to the spring air. "And that's
my vow to love you, Edie."

"So where are we going so fast?" she teased, looping
her arms tightly around his neck.

"To bed," Jimmy said simply.

"WE'VE STILL GOT A LOT to talk about," Jimmy's new wife
said the next evening, stretching her silken naked legs
against his and making him shudder. Without respond-
ing immediately, he flattened a palm and explored her
side, possessively enjoying the warmth of her skin, tracing a sloping breast, then the nip of her waist. Slowly,
he molded a hip and cupped the flesh, feeling a sudden
rush of heat flood into his groin.

Uttering a very soft, hungry male sound, he flexed
his back, arching toward her, his whole body coming
alive, every nerve ending zinging. Sucking a breath
through his clenched teeth, he could barely believe how
she made him feel. Even the hairs on his body seemed
to stand at attention, as if he'd just stuck his finger into
something electric, like a light socket.

And maybe he had. Because she was rolling on top
of him now, her straight blond hair cascading down-

ward, brushing his face and shoulders. Another wave of need claimed him, washing over his body like scalding water. Flexing his hands, he splayed his fingers wide and settled them on her back, lowering them slowly, so he could feel each vertebra before cupping her behind. Already, he knew she could tell how much he needed her, but he drew her closer, anyway, lifting his hips so she could feel him more fully. He was hard now, aching. And she was really his. Married to him. Forever.

"You know you have to do what I want now," he teased.

She sent him a mock-peeved look. "How's that?"

"Since we're married. There's no way out, except divorce. And I won't give you one."

She smiled. "You won't even let me talk about where we're going to live?"

He shook his head. "I've got other uses for your mouth."

"Like?"

"We need to talk about this," he murmured, his glazing eyes locking into hers as he urged her atop him, sighing in bliss as her knees parted beside his taut thighs, straddling him.

"Seriously. Where do you want to live?" she whispered.

"Here's good, at least for the moment," he offered, knowing he couldn't bear another moment of her teasing him. "My place is big enough for a bed. What more do you want?"

"Kitchen," she said.

"A demanding woman," he said. "I like that." Licking his lips against their dryness, he thrust a hand into her hair, guiding her face down for a kiss, the soft pressure of her lips increasing his desire, but not nearly as much as feeling her settle on top of where he wanted her most. *Inside,* he wanted to coax. But not now, not when her lips were parting and her tongue was toying with his, turning wetter and needier.

"We need a place for both of us," she whispered against his lips when she was done with a maddening, thorough kiss.

And they did. He was glad she liked his place, and particularly pleased that she was genuinely impressed, as others had been, by his more ambitious photography work, but it would never do for both of them. Already, he'd gotten in touch with some studios, thinking he'd segue back into attempting to have gallery shows by working in an art department. Maybe he'd even shoot a few weddings at Big Apple Brides for Edie. After all that had happened, she definitely needed help. This had turned out to be one of the world's most publicized weddings. Already, she was getting calls with new business.

Alone, Julia Darden's story, complete with its stalker, security risks and dogged photographer, had made for good copy. But now, people had wound up reporting the larger story, detailing the Benning wedding curse, the hidden relations between the Dardens and Bennings, and how Cash Champagne had been reunited with his biological father, as well as how the wedding had repaired relations for the Joneses. Melissa had vowed to give the money she'd earned to a charitable contribution, probably to the homeless shelter where Jack had stayed. She'd called Jimmy and Edie to say that if she was good for a year, her parents might still get her the horse.

The Stevenses story had been touching, too. Upon seeing the news in the *Post,* and realizing what Jack

Stevens had endured, how he really felt about his family, and how much he was trying to start a new life by checking himself into a rehab center, his wife and son had stepped forward to welcome him back home.

Yes. Maybe Jimmy would just become a full-time employee at Big Apple Brides. He was hardly intimidated by having a female boss, in fact, he'd invite it. He loved women. Especially Edie. A smile tilted his lips upward.

Unless, of course, Julia Darden had upstaged him as a photographer. Her picture of his and Edie's wedding had made the front page of the *Post*, after all. Because she'd attempted to get so many orders of pro- tection against him for snapping shots of her, the sense of irony had apparently appealed to everyone.

Unexpectedly, Emma Goldstein from *Celebrity Weddings* hadn't seemed all that angry about the turn of events, either, although she was to have had exclusive rights to take pictures. The wedding planner becoming the bride, she said, would have a certain appeal to her readership, as well. After all, Edie had wound up with her own dream wedding, one that only a man like Sparky Darden could have financed, and the involvement of her whole family made for a good human interest story.

Not to mention the fact that Pete Shriver had finally caught the writer of the poison-pen letters. After confiscating all the cameras at the rehearsal dinner, he'd promptly had the pictures developed and, as luck would have it, Melissa had accidently captured the culprit putting the letter into Lorenzo's pocket. Named Evan Enderson, he was one of Lorenzo's teammates who'd feared he'd wind up being cut from the team, unless Lorenzo wasn't included in the next year's lineup.

By targeting Julia, he'd hoped to cause Lorenzo stress that would affect his career.

There might have been some truth to the rumors regarding the team, too, according to sportscaster Tyrone Jones. Apparently, behind the scenes, Lorenzo's team managers had been considering cutting either Lorenzo or Evan by the next season. Now, given Evan Enderson's cutthroat tactics, the choice had been made for them. He'd been suspended until further notice, the implication being that he'd probably never come back.

All of which had only made Melissa more annoying than ever. After all, she was sure she was solely responsible for one of the *New York Post's* biggest stories of the year. Especially since her personal project—Jack Stevens—had turned out so well. Fortunately, Melissa's parents had wised up and were sticking closer to home, which meant Melissa was kept on a tighter leash and would be causing far less trouble in the future.

And if she wasn't, Jimmy would know. Pressured by Judge Diana Little, who said Jimmy owed her one since she'd agreed to leave her dinner parties and officiate over so many weddings, Jimmy had agreed to continue the community service project, teaching juveniles how to shoot pictures. Even though Melissa was finished with her sentence, she'd cut a special deal with Jimmy to sit in on his next class.

He sighed. Just a few hours ago, he'd put his parents back on a plane to Ohio, right after promising his mother he'd get right onto what both she and Vivian Benning had mapped out as his next important task— making them some grandbabies.

Which was exactly what Jimmy Delaney was now in the mood to do. But Edie was only staring down at him pointedly. "Can we stay in the Village? I mean, Mom and Dad live here…"

"Sure."

"Great," she gushed. "You really don't care?"

The only thing he cared about right now was burying his burning, aching flesh deep inside his wife. Shaking his head, he arched once more, using his fingers to guide her hips, showing her what he wanted. "I've got only one stipulation," he murmured throatily as he kissed her again.

"What?"

"It can't be your place. Because we're going to need a lot more room."

She frowned, her cheeks coloring, flushing with heat that he could feel seeping through her skin as she poised herself above him, then slowly lowered, sinking onto his rigid flesh, a movement that took their breath for a moment, so neither could talk. His chin tilted, his neck craning back in ecstasy.

"We are?"

Nodding, he brought his hands upward and caught her beautiful hair from beneath, letting strands fall through his splayed fingers as he massaged her scalp, gasping as she began to ride him. Abruptly, he pulled her down, his mouth searing on hers. "Yeah," he assured, "for the family we're going to make, Edie."

"Are you ready to do that now?" she whispered, her sparkling blue eyes assuring that her own thoughts matched his.

"Right now," he whispered back huskily, his voice breaking in the instant her lips found his again and his hips met the thrust of hers. "Let's fill our house, Edie Benning."

She couldn't have looked more pleased. Oh, yes, it was all synchronicity, he thought. Each moment was meant to be. They were both head people. Village people. Morning people. And now, they were going to be baby people, together, too.

"Yes," she murmured breathlessly, her excitement mounting, the velvet cream of her body enveloping him. "I think we're definitely on the same wavelength again."

Chuckling, Jimmy wrapped his arms tightly around her, hugging her close, and he simply said the only thing left to say, "I couldn't agree more."

* * * * *

If you enjoyed I THEE BED…,
make sure you catch…

Blaze # 181
UNDER HIS SKIN
by Jeanie London

kicking off the BIG EASY BAD BOYS *miniseries.*
Available this month.

How does an indecent proposal fit into a simple
business plan? Anthony DiLeo is about to find out.
When he approaches Tess Hardaway with an idea to
benefit both their companies, she counters with an
unexpected—and thoroughly steamy—
suggestion. A proposition that involves the two of
them getting to know each other in the
most intimate way!

1

"I WANT TESS HARDAWAY."

The statement came out sounding more like a demand than a request so Anthony DiLeo forced a smile at the guy behind the registration desk and tried again. "Is she around yet?"

"She was, but she left again."

"That's what you told me an hour ago."

"I know." The guy gave a lame shrug. "Sorry. You just keep missing her."

Anthony hoped like hell his bum timing didn't foreshadow the weekend ahead. Meeting Tess Hardaway was the only reason he'd come to Nostalgic Car Club's annual convention. He hadn't set eyes on her yet and already she'd given him the slip. Twice.

He tried not to look impatient. "You told me she'd be greeting people during registration."

"She has been. But she's also on the club's board—vice president of programming. She's been getting her presenters settled, too."

Okay, Tess Hardaway was a busy lady. He got that part. Anthony also got that this guy was nothing more than a volunteer. Obviously no one close to the elusive Tess Hardaway.

Anthony glanced down at the volunteer's name badge.

Timmy Martin, Montgomery, Alabama.

"All right, Timmy from Montgomery. Maybe you can tell me where to find Tess Hardaway since I'm not doing such a hot job tracking her down on my own."

"How about the CarTex Foundation's hospitality suite? Have you tried there yet?"

"Didn't know CarTex had a hospitality suite."

Timmy from Montgomery frowned. "Let me make a suggestion."

"Go."

"I know you wanted to register with Tess, but why don't you let me do the honors? I'll give you the registration packet and you can check out everything happening. Not only does CarTex have a hospitality suite, but they're hosting an event. Tess will be at both. If you want, I'll leave her a message."

"Yes, register. No, message."

No forewarning. But there might be a picture of her in the program. If he knew what the woman looked like, he could find her himself.

The guy nodded and got down to business. "Name?"

"Anthony DiLeo."

Timmy from Montgomery searched through file boxes filled with alphabetized folders. He withdrew one and skimmed through it.

"Everything's in order, Mr. DiLeo." He offered the folder. "This has your name badge, meal tickets, driving passes, room assignment and itinerary. This booklet has all the requirements for the weekend's events. That's important if you plan to participate in any of the races. You've got equipment requirements and paperwork to turn in."

"Got it." And Anthony did. He wanted Tess Hardaway and he'd gotten a convention package instead.

He *really* hoped this wasn't an omen.

After a pit stop at the front desk, he headed to his room to stow his gear.

The room was standard trendy. The hotel was standard trendy. The Chase Convention Center sat on the outskirts of Metairie, a stone's throw from New Orleans. Catering to traffic from the airport and Dixie Downs Speedway, the place was so close to Anthony's house he could have driven here nearly as fast as finding a free elevator to get down to the first floor.

But Tess Hardaway was in this hotel, and he'd waste valuable hunting time if he had to drive back and forth every day. He planned to make the most of every chance to cross her path this weekend.

Once he finally caught her.

Grabbing the program, Anthony sat on the edge of the bed and studied the hotel map to get a lay of the land. All the hospitality suites were located on the second floor.

Turning the program over, he wondered what an ad in here would cost. Hell, what about the price of hosting a weekend hospitality suite for twenty-six hundred guests?

Ten, twenty grand?

While he could have afforded to spend that kind of money on advertising, this wasn't his market. His business might have grown into the Big Easy's most reputed service and maintenance center in the years since he'd opened the doors, but no one would travel from Maine or Washington State to have their car serviced here.

Over the past few years, Anthony had watched CarTex become a big boy by expanding its operation, opening new service centers all over the nation, growing slowly, steadily, *successfully*. If he hooked up with Tess Hardaway, he'd take a step toward becoming a big boy, too.

With that thought, he rolled up the program, stuffed it into his back pocket and headed downstairs.

He found CarTex's hospitality suite easily enough. People had already begun milling around, glancing at the full-color promotional spreads detailing CarTex's unique philosophy on used vehicles as they worked their way toward the buffet.

Anthony wasn't interested in food. He was interested in the woman dressed in a dark blue business suit working the crowd.

Tess Hardaway?

He couldn't catch her name badge from this distance, but in that getup, she had to be with the company.

But as he neared the woman, Anthony second-guessed himself. From what he'd read about Tess Hardaway, he'd expected someone less…*suit*, precisely the reason he'd chosen her.

He waited. The woman didn't take long to direct her guests to the buffet, and when she did, she extended her hand to him.

"Penny Parker of CarTex." Her name badge read Marketing Director.

A *serious* suit.

"Anthony DiLeo of Anthony DiLeo Automotive."

She had an easy smile and a sharp gaze that took him in all at once. "A business owner. Local?"

He inclined his head.

"Please tell me you're not worried that CarTex's expansion into Louisiana will cut into your bottom line."

Anthony laughed. "I happen to respect smart business strategy, and Big Tex's makes sense. He has made reliable used transportation more accessible. I think that's a good thing."

"Even when we open an auto showroom in your backyard?"

"My service center is well-established in town. I don't have anything to worry about."

Her smile suggested she approved of his answer.

"All right, Anthony," she said with just enough drawl to tell him she was southern. "If you didn't come to pick my brain about our new showroom, then what can I do for you?"

"I'm looking for Tess Hardaway. I heard she'd be around."

"Really? Do you know Tess?"

"Not personally."

"I'm afraid you just missed her."

"I seem to be doing that a lot today."

That sharp gaze cut across him again.

"You don't happen to know where she went, do you?"

Penny leaned back on her stylish pumps and folded her arms across her chest. "Normally, I wouldn't dream of asking, but something about your interest is smacking me as more personal than professional. Why do you want to see Tess?"

"I'm sorry if I gave you that impression, Penny. My interest is strictly business. I came to this convention to network with Ms. Hardaway."

"Are you interested in the CarTex Foundation?"

"So to speak." That wasn't entirely true, but close enough. "I'd rather keep my business between me and Ms. Hardaway."

"Now I'm intrigued. Not even a hint?"

He spread his hands in entreaty. "Nothing mysterious. Just business."

From the look she gave him, he got the impression she couldn't quite make out what a local service center owner might want with the director of the CarTex Foundation. He also got the impression *her* interest was more than professional.

"She went to the speedway for the race."

"What race?" he asked. "I thought the convention didn't start until the welcome reception tonight."

"It doesn't *officially* start, but we always kick off with a low-speed race. Gets everyone in the mood. Tess wouldn't miss it for the world. Didn't you read your itinerary?"

"Not closely enough." He extended his hand. "A pleasure meeting you, Penny. Looks like I'm off to the races. I'm sure I'll run into you again."

She shook with a firm grip and gave him another easy smile. "If you don't catch up with her, try back here later."

"Thanks."

Anthony left the hotel optimistic that he might finally catch the woman who'd been eluding him all day. His optimism lasted until he reached the speedway ticket booth.

"Gates closed to the public," a grizzled man wearing a Dixie Downs uniform told him.

"I'm attending the convention."

"Name badge? Driving pass?"

Damn it. "In my hotel room. I didn't know I needed them."

"Can't let you through without your name badge and your driving pass."

"I won't be driving, just watching."

The gate didn't budge.

"When does the race start?"

The ticket taker glanced at his watch. "Ten minutes."

Not enough time to get to and from the hotel and still search the crowds for Tess Hardaway before the race began. He didn't think she'd be hard to find, though. Probably in the stands with the event hosts. "Can you call someone with the convention to verify I'm registered?"

"Call who?" the man asked gruffly, clearly not thrilled that Anthony intended to give him a hard time. Cocking his grizzled head toward the parking lot beyond the gate, he said, "The whole car club is inside for the race."

"The volunteer working the registration desk will confirm I'm with the convention—"

"Name badge and driving pass. It says so in the rules." He flourished a copy of the program.

"But I—"

"Name badge and driving pass," the ticket taker repeated stubbornly. "Or I call security."

Being labeled a gate-crasher by speedway security was *not* the first impression Anthony wanted to make with Big Tex's daughter. The success of his chosen career path now depended on her.

Scowling, he shifted his car into Reverse and backed away from the ticket booth. It wasn't until he'd almost reached the road that a sign caught his eye.

Drivers.

Anthony might not have belonged to a fancy car club like Nostalgic until he'd wanted to meet Tess Hardaway, but he'd been around cars since he could sit up straight enough to be strapped into his dad's vintage GTO.

Even more importantly, he'd been hanging around Dixie Downs for nearly as long. His first paying job had been in the pit working for a locally sponsored team. He knew his way around.

Without another thought, Anthony bypassed the gate and wheeled his car down the road leading to the track. He slid into the queue waiting to line up as if he belonged there.

When he reached the crewman in charge of registering the racers, he cranked down his window and said, "I'm looking for Tess Hardaway."

The guy didn't even look up over his clipboard. "The pole."

Well, well, well. He'd been wrong. Tess Hardaway wasn't in the stands, after all. She was lined up to race.

Leaning out his open window, he craned to see the course and spotted her immediately. One look and every bit of his inner car enthusiast cringed.

A *Gremlin?* A *purple* Gremlin.

He couldn't miss the florid paint, the custom parts or the jacked-up rear tires. The driver wore a matching purple helmet.

"Where's your gear?" The crewman had finally glanced up from his clipboard. "Can't give you a number without your gear."

"In the trunk." He'd expected to race sometime this weekend and now seemed as good a time as any to start. Hopping out, he circled his car, hoping he didn't need anything more than a helmet and gloves.

The crewman gave a nod. "We're running with the NCCC rule book. Helmet will work today, but if you want to race in Saturday's high-speed autocross, you'll need a fire suit."

"Got it."

The crewman must have assumed he'd shown his name badge and driving pass at the gate because he slapped a number 21 inside the windshield and waved him through. The next thing he knew, he slipped into the third row of the grid to wait for the pace car.

He finally had Tess Hardaway in sight.

Pulling on his helmet, he revved the engine to drown out the low-slung Corvette showing off in the slot beside him.

Anthony might not have raced in a while, but his foot slipped onto the gas pedal instinctively when the pace car appeared to lead them around the track for a parade lap. One by one, the cars pulled out to give the spectators a good look at the lineup.

Then came a pace lap before the official start of the race. The drivers traveled in formation, steadily increasing speed until they hit the ceiling before the starting line.

Then came the flag.

Anthony's adrenaline shot into gear with his engine. The Dixie Downs Speedway was his course. He knew the groove by heart—when to shut off to negotiate banked turns, what turns to ride the rails. He knew when to lean into the accelerator to gain distance through the chutes.

His Firebird took to the track as if he'd just raced her yesterday, and when the black Corvette tried to shut him out, Anthony diced a little, forcing the Corvette to back off.

He blew past with a laugh, his fingers easily gripping the steering wheel. He lapped the Corvette then sailed past a mint-condition Camaro. No contest. It had been too long since he'd done anything that had gotten his blood pumping.

Too damned long.

His fellow contestants didn't stand a chance. Anthony had a Gremlin to catch, and a driver leading the pack.

The feel of the track beneath his wheels and the silky way his car handled each turn brought back memories of the innumerable times he'd raced here. And each lap brought him closer to that purple hot rod.

Finally, he slipped into place behind her. After a few laps on her tail, Anthony admitted that not only did her funky little Gremlin pack more rpm grunt than he'd expected, but Tess Hardaway was one damned skilled driver. A little ruthless even.

She clearly enjoyed the thrill of the chase because she kept blipping to make him adjust his speed. Anthony let her play him for a bit. He'd intended to ride her bumper straight to the finish line. This woman would *not* get away again.

But the more she toyed with him, the harder he found it not to toy back.

Instinct finally took over. Slipping into her draft, he followed closely enough to take advantage of the decreased air resistance, so close that the chrome Gremlin character on her hatch grinned wickedly like a dare.

The race was on.

He sped up.

She slowed down.

He maneuvered the track.

She shut him out so he couldn't pass.

While Anthony might not have Tess Hardaway's maneuvers, he had the better car. And he put his Firebird to work when she fishtailed out of a hairy turn. She controlled the motion instantly—testimony to her skill—but skill was the only thing carrying her right now.

Instinct told him her hot rod was full out while his V-8 still had more to give. With a little more grunt and a lot of luck, he could maneuver past, well before that checkered flag came down to signal the end of the race.

Anthony had a split second to decide.

Whipping this woman's butt on the track hardly seemed a better introduction than being dragged in by security for crashing the gate.

But even more important than making a good first impression was a question: could Anthony live with himself if he let that prissy purple Gremlin whip his butt?

Silhouette® Desire®

**Coming in June 2005
from Silhouette Desire**

Emilie Rose's
SCANDALOUS PASSION

(Silhouette Desire #1660)

Phoebe Drew feared intimate photos
of her and her first love, Carter Jones,
would jeopardize her grandfather's
political career. So she went to Carter
for help finding them. But digging up
the past also uncovered long-hidden
passion, leaving Phoebe to wonder if
falling for Carter again would prove
to be her most scandalous decision.

*Available at your
favorite retail outlet.*

If you enjoyed what you just read,
then we've got an offer you can't resist!

Take 2 bestselling
love stories FREE!
Plus get a FREE surprise gift!

Clip this page and mail it to Harlequin Reader Service®

IN U.S.A.
3010 Walden Ave.
P.O. Box 1867
Buffalo, N.Y. 14240-1867

IN CANADA
P.O. Box 609
Fort Erie, Ontario
L2A 5X3

YES! Please send me 2 free Blaze™ novels and my free surprise gift. After receiving them, if I don't wish to receive anymore, I can return the shipping statement marked cancel. If I don't cancel, I will receive 4 brand-new novels each month, before they're available in stores! In the U.S.A., bill me at the bargain price of $3.99 plus 25¢ shipping and handling per book and applicable sales tax, if any*. In Canada, bill me at the bargain price of $4.47 plus 25¢ shipping and handling per book and applicable taxes**. That's the complete price and a savings of at least 10% off the cover prices—what a great deal! I understand that accepting the 2 free books and gift places me under no obligation ever to buy any books. I can always return a shipment and cancel at any time. Even if I never buy another book from Harlequin, the 2 free books and gift are mine to keep forever.

150 HDN DZ9K
350 HDN DZ9L

Name	(PLEASE PRINT)
Address	Apt.#
City	State/Prov.
	Zip/Postal Code

Not valid to current Harlequin Blaze™ subscribers.

Want to try two free books from another series?
Call 1-800-873-8635 or visit www.morefreebooks.com.

 * Terms and prices subject to change without notice. Sales tax applicable in N.Y.
** Canadian residents will be charged applicable provincial taxes and GST.
   All orders subject to approval. Offer limited to one per household.
 ® and ™ are registered trademarks owned and used by the trademark owner and or its licensee.

BLZ04R   ©2004 Harlequin Enterprises Limited.

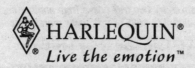

Silhouette®
Desire®

presents the next book in
Maureen Child's
miniseries

THREE WAY WAGER

*The Reilly triplets bet they could go
ninety days without sex. Hmm.*

WHATEVER
REILLY WANTS...
(Silhouette Desire #1658)
Available June 2005

All Connor Reilly had to do to win his no-sex-
for-ninety days bet was spend time with the
one woman who wouldn't tempt him. Yet
Emma Jacobsen had other plans, plans that
involved a *very* short skirt and a change
in attitude. Emma's transformation had
Connor forgetting about his wager—but
was what they had strong enough to last
more than ninety days?

Available at your favorite retail outlet.

HARLEQUIN® *Temptation*

AMERICAN HEROES

These men are heroes— strong, fearless... And impossible to resist!

Join bestselling authors Lori Foster, Donna Kauffman and Jill Shalvis as they deliver up

MEN OF COURAGE

Harlequin anthology
May 2003

Followed by *American Heroes* miniseries
in Harlequin Temptation

RILEY by Lori Foster
June 2003

SEAN by Donna Kauffman
July 2003

LUKE by Jill Shalvis
August 2003

Don't miss this sexy new miniseries by some of
Temptation's hottest authors!

Available at your favorite retail outlet.

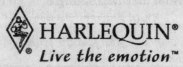

HARLEQUIN®
Live the emotion™

Visit us at www.eHarlequin.com

HTAH